BOY SCOUTS IN A SUBMARINE

OR, SEARCHING AN OCEAN FLOOR

G. HARVEY RALPHSON

1st WORLD
LIBRARY
Literary Society

Boy Scouts in a Submarine

G. Harvey Ralphson

© 1st World Library, 2009
PO Box 2211
Fairfield, IA 52556
www.1stworldlibrary.com
First Edition

LCCN: 2009923386

Softcover ISBN: 978-1-4218-8834-7
Hardcover ISBN: 978-1-4218-8933-7
eBook ISBN: 978-1-4218-8735-7

Purchase *"Boy Scouts in a Submarine"*
as a traditional bound book at:
www.1stWorldLibrary.com/purchase.asp?ISBN=978-1-4218-8834-7

1st World Library is a literary, educational organization
dedicated to:

- Creating a free internet library of downloadable ebooks

- Hosting writing competitions and offering book publishing
  scholarships.

Interested in more 1st World Library books? contact:
literacy@1stworldlibrary.com
Check us out at: www.1stworldlibrary.com

1ˢᵗ World Library Literary Society

Giving Back to the World

"If you want to work on the core problem, it's early school literacy."

- James Barksdale, former CEO of Netscape

"No skill is more crucial to the future of a child, or to a democratic and prosperous society, than literacy."

- Los Angeles Times

"Literacy... means far more than learning how to read and write... The aim is to transmit... knowledge and promote social participation."

- UNESCO

"Literacy is not a luxury, it is a right and a responsibility. If our world is to meet the challenges of the twenty-first century we must harness the energy and creativity of all our citizens."

- President Bill Clinton

"Parents should be encouraged to read to their children, and teachers should be equipped with all available techniques for teaching literacy, so the varying needs and capacities of individual kids can be taken into account."

- Hugh Mackay

CONTENTS

CHAPTER I

LOST ON AN OCEAN FLOOR

The handsome clubroom of the Black Bear Patrol, Boy Scouts of America, in the City of New York, was ablaze with light, and as noisy as healthy, happy boys could well make it.

"Over in the Chinese Sea!" shouted Jimmie McGraw from a table which stood by an open window overlooking the brilliantly illuminated city. "Do we go to the washee-washee land this time?"

"Only to the tub!" Jack Bosworth put in.

"What's the answer?" asked Frank Shaw, sitting down on the edge of the table and rumpling Jimmie's red hair with both hands.

Jimmie broke away and, after bouncing a football off his tormentor's back, perched himself on the back of a great easy chair.

"The answer?" Jack said, after peace had been in a measure restored, "I thought everybody knew that the Chinks wash their clothes in the Gulf of Tong King and hang them out to dry on the mountains of Kwang Tung! Are we going there,

Ned?" he added, turning to Ned Nestor, who sat by a nearby window, looking out over the city. "Are we going to the gulf of Tong King?"

Ned left his chair by the window and walked over to the table.

"I hardly know," he said, taking a roll of maps and drawings from his breast pocket and spreading them out on the table. "When Captain Moore arrives we shall know more about it."

"Who's Captain Moore?"

This from Jimmie, still sitting on the back of the chair, elbows on knees, chin on palms.

"Is he going to be the big noise?"

This from Jack Bosworth, who was reaching out with his foot in a vain effort to tip Jimmie's chair and send him sprawling.

"Is Captain Moore going with us?"

This question was asked by Frank Shaw with a show of anxiety. When out on their trips the Boy Scouts did not relish having older men about to show authority.

"One question at a time!" laughed Ned. "To answer the first query first, Captain Moore is the Secret Service officer who is to post us with regard to our mission to Chinese waters. Second he will, to use the slang adopted by Jack, be the 'Big Noise' as long as he is with us. Third, I don't know whether he is going on the journey with us or not."

"Here's hopin' he don't!" cried Jimmie.

G. Harvey Ralphson

"He'll want us to sit in baby chairs at tables and object to our takin' moonlight walks on the bottom of the sea! Is he covered all over with brass buttons, an' does he strut like this?"

Jimmie bounded to the floor and walked up and down the room with a mock military stride which set his companions into roars of laughter.

"I have never seen him," Ned replied. "He is coming here tonight, and you must judge for yourself what kind of a man he is."

"Here?" asked Frank. "Here to this club-room? The boys won't do a thing to him if he puts on dog!"

"Is he a submarine expert?" asked Frank.

"Sure!" replied Jack. "He wouldn't be sent here to post us if he wasn't, would he?"

"I don't believe he knows any more about a submarine, right now, than Ned does," Jimmie exclaimed. "Ned's been taking walks on the bottom of the Bay every mornin' for a week!"

Jack and Frank turned to Ned with amazement showing on their faces.

"Have you, Ned?" they asked, in chorus.

"Have you been out training without letting us know about it?"

"You bet he has!" Jimmie grinned. "I've been with him most of the time too. This Captain Moore, whoever he is, hain't got nothin' on Ned when it comes to makin' the wheels go round under the water."

"Oh, you!" laughed Jack, pointing a finger at Jimmie. "You can't run a submarine, even if Ned can."

"You wait an' see!" retorted the boy, indignantly. "You wait until we get into the Chinese sea, then you'll see what I know about boats that travel on ocean beds!"

"Can he run a submarine, Ned?" asked Jack.

"Well," was the laughing reply, "he did pretty well on the last trip. If some one hadn't interfered with his steering I reckon he would have tipped the Statue of Liberty into the Atlantic!"

Jimmie winked when the others roared at him and then looked reproachfully at Ned.

"You promised not to tell about that!" he said, accusingly.

At that moment a knock came on the door of the clubroom, which was on the top of the palatial residence of Jack Bosworth's father, and a moment later a tall, military-looking man with a white, stern face, thin straight lips and cold blue eyes was shown in. He paused just outside the doorway, and the boy who did not catch the sneer on his chalky face as he looked superciliously over the group must have been very unobservant indeed.

"Gee! He don't seem to like the looks of us!" Jimmie whispered to Frank Shaw, as Ned stepped forward to greet the newcomer.

"Looks like a false alarm!" Frank replied, in an aside. "I hope we don't have to lug him along with us."

"We won't need any cold storage arrangement on the submarine if he does go!" Jimmie went on. "That face of his would freeze hot steel."

Captain Moore of the United States Secret Service remained standing near the door until Ned reached his side. Then he lifted a single glass, inserted it in his eye-orbit and stood gazing at the boy who had advanced to welcome him.

Ned stepped back, coldly, and Jimmie nudged Jack delightedly when he saw the lad's face harden into bare civility.

"Aw," began the visitor, "I'm looking for—ah!—Mr. Nestor!"

"I'm Ned Nestor," said the boy, shortly.

"Fawncy!"

Ned pointed toward the table where the other boys were sitting and moved away.

"Fawncy!" repeated the visitor.

Ned made no reply. Instead, he marched to the table, drew a chair forward, and motioned Captain Moore to be seated.

Before complying with this gracious invitation the Captain glanced around the apartment with the supercilious sneer he had shown on entering. The boys watched him with heavy frowns on their faces.

"If we've got to take this along in the submarine," Jimmie whispered to Jack, "I hope the boat will drop down into a deep hole and stay there. Look at it!"

"Hush!" whispered the other. "It has ears!"

Those who have read the first and second volumes of this series will understand without being told here that it was a very fine clubroom upon which the frosty blue eyes of the Secret Service man looked.

The walls were adorned with all manner of hunting and fishing paraphernalia, together with many trophies of the chase. Foils, gloves, ball bats, paddles and many other athletic aids were scattered about the large room.

This clubroom, that of the Black Bear Patrol, as has been said, was the handsomest in New York, the members of the Patrol being sons of very wealthy men. The father of Frank Shaw was editor and owner of one of the important daily newspapers of the metropolis. Jack Bosworth's father was a prominent corporation lawyer, while Harry Stevens, a lad with a historical hobby, was a prominent automobile manufacturer.

Ned Nestor, the boy just now trying to entertain the very formal Captain Moore, was a member of the Wolf Patrol, also of New York, as was also Jimmie McGraw, who had been a Bowery newsboy before joining fortunes with Ned.

As is well known to most of our readers, Ned had, at one time and another, undertaken and successfully accomplished delicate and hazardous enterprises for the United States Government. Accompanied by Frank, Jack, Jimmie, Harry, and other members of the Boy Scout Patrols of the United States, he had visited Mexico, the Canal Zone, the Philippines, the Great Northwest, had navigated the Columbia river in a motor boat, and had covered the continent of South America in an aeroplane.

G. Harvey Ralphson

He was now about to enter upon, perhaps, the most important mission ever assigned to him by the Secret Service department. The story of the quest upon which he was about to enter will best be told in the conversation which now took place in the clubroom of the Black Bear Patrol on this evening of the 11th of September.

Presently Captain Moore transferred his gaze from the apartment to the boys gathered about the table and grouped about the place. As a matter of course all conversation in the room had ceased on the arrival of the Captain. While the boys who were not fortunate enough to be planning on the trip in the submarine were too courteous to openly stare at their guest of the moment, it may well be believed that his every look and word was closely noted.

Concluding his rather rude observations, Captain Moore dropped his glass, shrugged his shoulders, which were heavily padded, and gave utterance to his feelings in the one word of comments which he had twice used before:

"Fawncy!"

Ned said not a word, but waited for the visitor to lead out in the talk. Captain Moore was in no haste to begin, but he finally broke the silence by asking:

"You are Ned Nestor?"

Ned bowed stiffly. He did not like the man he was supposed to do business with, and did not try to conceal the fact.

"The Ned Nestor who undertook the Secret Service work in the Canal Zone and South America?"

Ned nodded again.

"Fawncy!"

"You said that before?" broke in Jimmie, who was fuming under the idea that the Captain was not treating his chum with proper courtesy.

The Captain brought his glass into use again and looked the boy over, much as he would have inspected a curio in a museum. Jimmie glared back, and the eyes of the two fenced for a moment before a twinkle of humor appeared in those of the Captain.

"You are Jimmie, eh?" the latter demanded.

Jimmie would have made some discourteous reply only for the tug Ned gave at his sleeve. As it was he only nodded.

"Aw, I've heard of you!" the Captain said, then. "Quite remarkable—quite extraordinary!"

"You came to deliver instructions regarding the submarine trip?" Ned asked, feeling revolt in the air of the room.

Unless something was done, the boys, all resenting the manner of the Captain, would be beyond control, and then the Secret Service man would be likely to leave the place in anger.

This, in turn, might endanger the adventure already planned and prepared for, for the chief of the department might see fit to adopt whatever recommendations Captain Moore made in the matter.

The visitor might have sensed the hostility, for he hastened to take from a pocket a sheaf of papers and place them on the table. The next moment the boys all saw that they had not

G. Harvey Ralphson

gained a correct estimate of the Secret Service man.

The instant he began talking of the matter which had brought him to the clubroom his manner changed. He was no longer the drawling, supercilious naval officer in resplendent uniform. He was a keen-brained mechanical expert, questioning Ned regarding his knowledge of submarines.

"You are fairly well up in the matter," the Captain said, going back to his old drawl, in a few moments. "I shall not object to your going on the Diver with me."

The boys all gasped. So their worst fears were coming true! The Captain was indeed going with them! He would be the commander, and Ned would be obliged to work under his orders if he went at all!

Would Ned do this? Would he submit to the authority of another while practically responsible for the results of the trip? Frank, Jack, and Jimmie saw their cherished plans go glimmering.

Ned made no reply whatever. Instead he began asking questions concerning the Diver as the submarine the Captain had in view was named, and also about the object of the expedition.

"A short time ago," the Captain said, "the Cutaria, a fast mail boat, went down in the Gulf of Tong King, carrying with her many passengers, the United States mails, and $10,000,000 in gold consigned to the Chinese Government. We are to search the ocean floor for the gold, and also for information sought by the Department of State."

"Who got careless and dropped $10,000,000 on an ocean floor?" asked Jimmie.

CHAPTER II

A CONFLICT OF AUTHORITY

The Captain gazed at Jimmie for a moment without answering. Then he parted his thin lips and uttered the old, familiar word:

"Fawncy!"

"The Cutaria went down as the result of a collision?" Ned hastened to ask, observing that Jimmie was growing flushed and angry.

"Yes," was the reply, "and it is asserted in the diplomatic circles of foreign governments that she was rammed by the orders of a power alleged to be friendly to our Government, and that our department of state does not dare remonstrate and ask for reparation for the reason that an investigation would reveal the fact that the $10,000,000 in gold which was lost was not really, as alleged, on its way from the sub-treasury in New York to the treasurer of the Chinese Empire."

"But why should Uncle Sam be sending money over there?" asked Ned.

G. Harvey Ralphson

"It is asserted that the money was sent at the command of men high in influence in Washington who understood that it was to be seized while in transit, after reaching Chinese soil, and used to assist the radical fomentation now going on in China."

"An indirect way, a sly and underhand way, of assisting the revolutionary party in China to get control of the government, eh?" asked Ned.

"Aw, that is what is claimed," was the reply.

"And you are to have charge of the expedition?" asked Ned, quietly, his eyes fixed keenly on the face of the visitor.

"Orders," was the slow reply.

"And the Diver has been chosen as the boat?"

"At my request, yes."

"But," Ned then said, by way of protest, "I have made all my trial trips in the Sea Lion."

"You will soon learn to help handle the Diver," was the lofty reply.

"The Diver is no more like the Sea Lion than she is like the Ark," was Ned's reply. "It will take me another fortnight to learn to run her, I'm afraid."

"You can take lessons from my son on the way over," was the unsatisfactory reply.

"Why, the submarine is not going to sail across the Pacific," said the boy. "As I understand it, we are to take passage in a mail steamer at San Francisco and find the submarine in some harbor of the island of Hainan, after she arrives on the other side in a man-of-war which will be detailed to carry her over."

"I have changed all that," said the Captain.

Ned said no more on that phase of the matter at that time, but the boys knew that he had not given up his original intention of making the explorations in the Sea Lion, the submarine which the Secret Service chief at New York had placed at his disposal soon after his return from South America.

"You will be permitted to take one of your—ah, Boy Scouts with you," the Captain went on. "Baby bunch, the Boy Scouts, what?" he added, lifting his glass and surveying the boys grouped about in a manner which brought the hot blood to their cheeks.

"I'm afraid you have never investigated the Boy—"

Ned's conciliatory remark was cut short by Jimmie.

"Will the Boy Scout who goes with him be allowed to breathe?" the boy asked.

Captain Moore eyed the lad critically through his glass.

"You needn't concern yourself about that, bub," he said, after an exasperating silence, "for you won't be the one to go, don't you know—not the Boy Scout to go."

Jimmie was about to make some angry reply, but Frank seized him by the arm and marched him to a distant part of the large room.

"You'll queer the whole thing!" Frank said.

Jimmie shook himself free of the detaining hand and faced the Captain with flashing eyes.

"I don't care if I do!" he said. "That thing is not going to make ugly remarks about the Boy Scouts without bein' called for it. He's an old false alarm, anyway. I'll bet he never heard a real gun go off!"

Captain Moore heard the insulting words and arose.

"If you'll, aw, come to my office tomorrow morning," he said, to Ned, "we'll discuss the, aw, mattah. I cawn't remain here and quarrel with boys who ought to be, aw, spanked and put, aw, to bed as soon as the sun goes down."

Ned did not rise from his chair to escort the Captain to the door. His face was pale and there was a dangerous light in his eyes.

"It won't be necessary for me to visit you in the morning," he said.

The Captain fixed his glass.

"Fawncy!" he exclaimed.

"Anything you like!" Ned said.

"Fawncy!" repeated the Captain.

"As you please," Ned smiled. "Fawncy anything you like— anything agreeable, you know."

"And why won't you come to my office in the morning?"

asked the Captain, with a tightening of his thin lips.

"I have decided to withdraw from the enterprise," was the quiet reply. "I'm out of it."

The boys gathered about Ned with cheers and words of encouragement.

"Go it, old boy!" cried one.

"Don't let him bluff you!" cried another.

"Dad will buy you a submarine!" Frank Shaw put in.

The Captain stood in the middle of the group, gazing in perplexity from face to face.

"My word!" he said, presently.

"What about it?" asked Jimmie, edging closer.

"Not going?" continued the Captain; "why?"

"I've changed my mind," was the unsatisfactory reply.

"But the submarine is waiting," urged the Captain.

"I shall never go to the bottom in the Diver," Ned replied.

"My word!"

The Captain loitered, as if anxious to reopen the whole matter, but Ned turned his back and seemed inclined to consider the case closed.

"And so we're not going?" asked Frank.

"Rotten shame!" declared Jack.

"So fades me happy, happy dream!" chanted Jimmie.

The Captain stuck his glass in his eye and moved toward the door, an expression of satisfaction on his stern face.

No one opened the door for him, and when he opened it for himself, he found a slender, middle-aged man with a pleasant face and brilliant eyes confronting him. His supercilious manner vanished instantly, and the military cap he had already donned came off with a jerk.

"Admiral!" he exclaimed.

The boys gathered about the doorway, all excitement. A real, live admiral in the Boy Scout clubroom! That was almost too much to expect.

The admiral saluted and stepped inside the room.

"Pardon me," he said, addressing Ned rather than the Captain, "but I must confess that I have been doing a discourteous thing. I have been listening at your door."

"I sincerely hope you heard all that was said," the Captain ventured. "I have been shamefully insulted here."

"Did you hear all that was said?" asked Nestor.

The Admiral bowed.

"I think so," he said.

"I'm glad of that," Frank said, "for this Captain does not tell the truth."

Captain Moore frowned in the direction of the speaker but said not a word.

"When I reached the door," the Admiral said, "I heard Captain Moore saying that the trip was to be made in the Diver, and that he was to have charge."

"That is the way I understand it," Captain Moore hastened to say. "And," continued the Admiral, "he said, further, that only one Boy Scout would be permitted to accompany Mr. Nestor."

"That will be quite enough, judging from the samples we see here," the Captain observed, with a vicious glance toward Jimmie, whose face was now set in a broad grin.

"Those are the statements made by Captain Moore," Ned said. "I refused to accept them."

"Quite right!" said the Admiral.

Captain Moore stuck his glass in his eye again and, saluting, turned toward the door.

"Wait!" commanded the Admiral.

The angry Captain turned back, a scowl on his face.

"Mr. Nestor," the Admiral continued, "goes in charge of the expedition, and in the Sea Lion, the submarine he has been experimenting with. He will be permitted to take three of his companions with him. Any officer who goes in the Sea Lion will necessarily remain under Mr. Nestor's orders."

"Then I ask for a transfer," scowled the Captain.

"Granted," answered the Admiral. "You may go now."

Captain Moore lost no time getting out of the door, and then the Admiral seated himself and motioned Ned to do likewise. The boys gathered about, but Ned asked them to proceed with their sports, and only the ex-newsboy remained at the table.

"I'm sorry to say," the Admiral began, "that there are hints of the most despicable disloyalty and treachery in this matter. I don't like to cast suspicions on Captain Moore, who really is an expert submarine officer, but it appears to me that he went beyond his authority in changing the plans for the cruise."

"He had no authority for changing from the Sea Lion to the Diver?" asked Ned.

"Not the slightest."

"Or for changing from a steamer ride to China to a long journey on the submarine?"

"Not at all."

"But he was sent here by the Secret Service department to instruct me," Ned said.

"Exactly, and that is all he was expected to do in the case. I don't understand his conduct."

Jimmie, who had been looking over an afternoon newspaper which lay on the table, now broke into the conversation.

"Just look here," he said. "This tells why Captain Moore butted into the game wrong. Just read that."

The Admiral took the newspaper into his hand and read, aloud:

"The Diver, the famous submarine boat invented by Arthur Moore, the talented son of Captain Henry Moore, of the United States navy, is soon to be put in commission for a most extraordinary voyage. Under the command of Captain Moore, who will be accompanied by the inventor, his son, the Diver will make the trip from San Francisco to China, almost entirely under water. It is understood that the submarine goes on secret service for the Government."

"There you are!" cried Jimmie.

"I rather think that does explain a lot," laughed Ned.

"The Diver," said the Admiral, thoughtfully, "has not yet been accepted by the Government, and I see trouble ahead for the Sea Lion."

CHAPTER III

"THE DANDY SUBMARINE"

The Sea Lion was a United States submarine, yet she was not constructed along the usual naval lines. It was said of her that she looked more like a pleasure yacht built for under-surface work than anything else.

It is not the purpose of the writer to enter into a minute description of the craft. She was provided with a gasoline engine and an electric motor. She was not very roomy, but her appointments were very handsome and costly.

There were machines for manufacturing pure air, as is common with all submarines of her class, and the apparatus for the production of electricity was modern and efficient. Every compartment could be closed against every other chamber in case of damage to the shell.

The pumps designed to expel the water taken into the hold for the purpose of bringing the craft to the bottom were powerful, so that she seemed to sink and rise as easily as does a bird on the wing. At top speed she would make about twenty miles an hour.

On a trial trip taken by Ned on the day before the visit of

Captain Moore to the Black Bear clubroom, the double doors and closet which enabled one to leave or enter the boat while under water had been thoroughly tested and found to work perfectly.

The diving suits—which had been manufactured to fit Ned and Frank, Jack and Jimmie—were also found to be in perfect condition.

On the whole, the Sea Lion and her appurtenances were in as perfect condition as science and experience could make them on the day the four boys, accompanied by a naval officer, left the train at Oakland and proceeded to the navy yard up the bay.

By the middle of the afternoon the boys were on board, receiving their final instructions from Lieutenant Scott, who had arranged for the transportation of the Sea Lion from New York and attended to all other details connected with the trip.

After a long talk regarding the perils to be encountered, Lieutenant Scott drew forth a map of peculiar appearance and laid it on the table in the chamber which was to serve as a general living room.

"I have retained possession of this map until the last moment," the officer said, "because it is most important that no eyes but those of the occupants of the Sea Lion should rest upon it. It shows where the lost vessel went down, shows the drift there, the depths, and various other details of great moment.

"The Cutaria, as you doubtless know, went down off the Taya Islands, a small group to the east of the large island of Hainan, which, in turn, is off the coast of China, being separated, if that is a good word to use in this connection, from the eastern coast by the Gulf of Tong King.

"Immediately following the sinking of the ship divers were sent down. They found the lost ship resting easily in about sixty feet of water. A few days later, however, when other divers went down, the wreck was not at the place described by the first operators.

"There are drift currents there, but it is remarkable that so heavy a wreck should have been shifted so suddenly. There are no indications that the vessel has been buried in the sands of the bottom. Your duty is to search the ocean floor then and locate the wreck. Having done this you are to secure the treasure, if possible. In case you cannot do this, you are to steam to Hongkong and report what assistance you require.

"And remember this: You are not to destroy or mislay any documents you may find in the gold room. You are not to reveal the purpose of your mission at any port you may touch on the way out, or at any port you may visit for the purpose of reporting progress.

"If at any time you have reason to believe that another submarine is working or loitering about in the vicinity of the wreck, you are to report the fact without delay and a man-of-war will be sent to you."

"And that means—"

Ned did not complete the sentence, for the officer hastened to explain the meaning of the warning.

"The Diver," he said, "is somewhere on this coast."

Ned gave a quick start of surprise.

"I knew it!" shouted Jimmie. "I just knew we were in for somethin' of the kind! There'll be doin's."

"I reckon we can take care of the Diver," said Frank, "and Mr. Arthur Moore, son of Captain Henry Moore, with it."

"Don't underestimate the Diver," warned Lieutenant Scott. "She is a peach of a submarine, and Mr. Arthur Moore knows how to operate her. She is almost the latest thing in submarines."

"Why didn't the Government buy her, then?" demanded Jack.

"Principally because she was withdrawn from the market," was the reply.

"I begin to understand," Ned said.

"Then that son of Captain Moore is after the gold?" asked Jack.

"That is what we suspect."

"Well," Frank said, then, "it wouldn't be any fun to go after the old wreck if all was clear sailing."

"Right you are!" cried Jimmie.

"But how did they get the Diver here so quickly?" asked Ned.

"The same way I got the Sea Lion here," was the Lieutenant's reply. "They engaged a special train, took the boat to pieces as far as practicable and sent her over."

"But she is something of a whale as compared with the little

Sea Lion," urged Ned. "It was easy enough to get our boat across the continent."

"Not quite so easy as you think," laughed the officer. "Still," he added, "here she is, all ready for the trip. There are plenty of provisions, and everything is in fine working order. You, Mr. Nestor, took a hand in taking the submarine to pieces, and you ought to know all about her."

"I think I do," was the reply, "still, I should have liked the chance of putting her together again."

"It is all right as it is," was the reply. "You doubtless had a good time in New York while the work was being done here. When I left for the big city to ride over with you she was nearly ready, and now, on our arrival, she is, as you see, right and fit."

"But I thought we were to cross the Pacific in a steamer and pick up the Sea Lion over there," Ned observed.

"Right you are," the Lieutenant answered, "but the Sea Lion is to be taken over by the big steamer, too."

"Then they've got to take her to pieces again," wailed Jimmie, "and it will be weeks before we get started."

"You are wrong there," the officer replied. "The Sea Lion will be picked up by something like a floating dock and towed over. How does that strike you?"

"Out of water?" asked Frank.

"Of course. Novel way of carrying a submarine, eh?"

"I should say so."

"Over there," the Lieutenant went on, "there would be no facilities for assembling the parts. That is why the work was done here."

"Of course," laughed Frank.

"And this floating dry dock," continued the officer, "will be roofed over and its contents kept secret. A short distance from the Taya Islands, she will be shucked of her shell and take to the water. No one will know what her mission is."

"It seems to me that everything is pretty cleverly planned," Ned remarked. "I hope all my plans will come together as nicely as the plans of the Government have."

"That will be a big tow for a steamer," Jimmie suggested.

"Yes, it is awkward, but there seemed to be no other way. The Diver will be far in the rear and you take water off the Taya Islands."

"And on the way over," Ned said, "I can live in the Sea Lion and continue my studies of the machinery."

"That is the idea," said the Lieutenant.

"When are we to be picked up?" asked Jack.

The Lieutenant lifted a hand for silence.

From outside, seemingly from underneath the keel of the Sea Lion, came a grating sound, which was followed by a slight, though steady, lifting of the vessel.

"Gee!" cried Jimmie, springing to his feet. "I guess we're up against an earthquake!"

The boys were all moving about now, but Lieutenant Scott remained in his chair, a smile on his face.

The Sea Lion rose steadily, and there was a slight tip to port. Ned sat down with a shamed look on his face.

"I should have known," he said.

"Say," Jack exclaimed, "was the submarine put together on the float that is going to carry her across?"

"Of course she was," laughed the Lieutenant. "The pieces brought on from New York were assembled on the float. Some of the larger pieces, the ones most difficult to handle, were made here from patterns sent on from the east. Then, when all was ready, the float was dropped out of sight so the submarine would lie on the surface, as we found her."

"And now they're lifting the float?" asked Jimmie.

"Exactly," was the reply. "Suppose you go outside, on the conning tower, and look about."

"You bet," cried Jack, and then there was a rush for the stairway, or half-ladder, rather, leading to the tower.

The Sea Lion was still lifting, though where the power came from no one could determine. While Ned studied over the problem Lieutenant Scott laid a hand on his shoulder.

"You want to know what makes the wheels go round?" laughed the officer. "Well, I'll tell you. The bottom of the float forms a tank. Now do you see?"

"And there's a large hose laid from the tank to the shore, and the water is being pumped out! I see."

"That's it," replied the Lieutenant. "Now that we are getting up high and dry, you boys can step down on the floor of the float and look about. I don't think there was ever a contrivance exactly like this. Go and look it over."

Night was falling, and a chill October wind was blowing in from the Pacific. There were banks of clouds, too, and all signs portended rain. It would be a dismal night.

Leaving Lieutenant Scott in the conning tower, the boys all clambered down to the floor of the float to examine the blockings which kept the submarine on a level keel. They were gone only a short time, but when they climbed up the rope ladder to the conning tower again the light was dim, and a slow, cold rain was falling. The Lieutenant was not on the conning tower, and Ned at once descended to the general living room of the submarine. Before he reached the middle of the stairs the lights, which had been burning brightly a moment before, suddenly went out, and the interior of the submarine yawned under his feet like a deep, impenetrable pit.

Fearful that something was amiss, Ned dropped down and reached for his electric searchlight, which he had left on a shelf not far from the stairs. Something passed him in the darkness and he called out to the Lieutenant, but there was no answer. Then, out of the darkness above, came a mingled chorus of anger and alarm.

CHAPTER IV

A WOLF ON THE TRAIL

"That isn't Ned!" cried Jack's voice, in a moment.

"Don't let him get away! He's been up to some mischief!"

That was Frank Shaw's voice.

"Soak him!"

That could be no one but Jimmie!

Ned, groping about in the darkness, heard the voices faintly. He seemed to be submerged in a sweep of pounding waves, the steady beating of which shut out all individual sounds.

He knew that he staggered and stumbled as he walked. Moving across the floor his feet came in contact with some soft obstruction lying on the rug and he fell down.

There was a strange, choking odor in the place, and he groped on his hands and knees in the direction of the shelf where his searchlight had been left. His senses reeled, and for an instant he lay flat on the floor.

Then he heard the boys clambering down the stairs from the conning tower and called out, feebly, yet with sufficient strength to make himself heard above the sound of shuffling feet.

"Go back!" he cried. "Don't come in here! Leave the hatch open, and let in air. Go back!"

Jimmie recognized a note of alarm, of suffering, in the voice of his chum and dropped headlong into the black pit of the submarine. Ned heard him snap the catch of a searchlight, and then, dimly, heard his voice:

"Gee!" the voice said. "What's comin' off here?"

The round face of the electric searchlight showed at the end of a cylindrical shaft of light which rested on Ned's face, but the boy did not realize what was going on until he felt a gust of wind and a drizzle of rain on his forehead.

Then he opened his eyes to find himself on the conning tower of the submarine, with the boys gathered about him, anxiety showing in their speech and manner. It was too dark for him to see their faces.

"You're all right now," Jimmie said. "What got you down there?"

Then Ned remembered the sudden extinction of the lights as he moved down the stairs, the stifling, choking odor below, and the deadly grip of suffocation which had brought him to the floor.

"Go back into the boat," he said, gaining strength every moment. "I am anxious about Lieutenant Scott."

"We've just come from there," Frank said. "We've done all that can be done for him."

"What do you mean by that?" demanded Ned, moving toward the hatch which sealed the submarine.

"The poison which keeled you over got him!" Jack said.

"Do you mean that he's dead?" asked Ned, a shiver running through his body as he spoke.

"I'm afraid so," was the reply. "We got you out just in time. You would have perished in a moment more."

"Dead!" said Ned. "Lieutenant Scott dead! And he was so gay and so full of life a few moments ago!"

Jack, who had left the little group a moment before, now returned.

"The poison seems to have evaporated from the interior," he said, "so we may as well go below. I'll go ahead and turn on the lights." The body of the naval officer lay in a huddle at the foot of the stairs leading to the conning tower, just far enough to the rear so that the free passage was not obstructed. With all the lights turned on and every aperture which might transmit a ray to the world outside closed, the boys, after placing the body on a couch, began a close examination of the boat.

There were no wounds on the body, so it seemed that he had died from suffocation. There was still a sickening odor in the boat, but the constant manufacture of fresh air was gradually doing away with this.

The door to the room where the dynamos and the gasoline

engine were situated was found wide open, and Ned instructed the boys to leave it so and leave everything untouched.

"The first thing to do," he said, "is to discover any clues the assassin may have left here. It is an old theory that no person, however careful he or she may be, can enter and leave a room without leaving behind some evidence of his or her presence there. We'll soon know if this is true in this case."

"There was some one in here, all right," Jimmie said. "He passed us on the conning tower, skipping like to break the speed limit for the city. I tried to trip him as he passed me, an' got this."

The lad turned a bruised face toward his companions. In the confusion no one had observed the cut on his cheek.

"You did get something!" Jack exclaimed. "Why didn't you say something about it?"

"Nothin' doin'!" answered the boy. "Only a scratch!"

Notwithstanding the boy's claim that the wound was of small importance, Ned insisted on its being dressed at once.

"Now," Ned said, after the cut had been properly cared for, "what sort of a man was it that passed you boys on the conning tower? The circular platform is so small that he must have crowded you pretty closely when he stepped out."

"He did," Jimmie answered. "I thought it was you, and stepped aside to make room for him."

"And then?"

"I had a feeling that it wasn't you. Then, he was makin' for the wharf so fast that I thought it would do no harm to have a look at him, and so called out."

"Then's when you got the slash across the cheek?"

"Yes; he cut me then."

"What about the size of the fellow?" asked Ned.

"Oh, I should think he was slender and light, the way he bounded off the platform and made for the wharf."

"Do you think he went there to kill Lieutenant Scott?" asked Jack, a moment later.

"It is more probable that he came here to put the Sea Lion out of commission," Frank replied.

"I'll bet well find somethin' all busted up!" Jimmie predicted.

"Ned can soon determine that," Jack remarked.

"Yes," Ned went on, "but the first thing to do is to see if this murderer left any visiting cards here. After that, we must notify the Coroner and have the body removed."

Ned went into the dynamo room and looked about.

"Here is where any enemy would have to do his work," he said, "so we must look for clues here. Keep your hands off the machinery, for he may have left finger marks some-where."

Ned searched long and carefully without reward. Finally he turned to the waiting boys.

"There's quite a lot of waste lying around," he said. "Secure every fiber of it and examine it under the microscope. You would better attend to that, Frank, as you are familiar with the instrument. If you discover anything foreign to a place like this, let me know."

While Ned continued his search about the interior of the submarine, Frank busied himself inspecting the bits of waste the other boys brought to him. At last an exclamation of astonishment brought Ned to his side.

"There's something funny about this," Frank said, as Ned bent over his shoulder. "That stuff is not oil, and I'd like to know how it got in here."

"What does it look like?" asked Ned.

"I can't say," was the hesitating reply.

Ned took the microscope and looked at the object to which his attention had been called.

"Rubber!" he said, in a moment.

"Rubber!" repeated Frank. "How could rubber be in the waste in that shape?"

"All the same," Ned replied, "this is some rubber composition, and it has been wiped into the waste. Now, what could any person want with rubber here?"

"It is used quite a lot around electric apparatus," suggested Frank Shaw.

"But not in this form," Ned replied.

Then, remembering certain smooth blurs on the polished machinery he had recently examined, he took the microscope and made another examination of the spots. Presently he called Frank to his side.

"Look through the glass," he said, handing the instrument to Frank, "and tell me what you see."

"Rubber!" cried the boy, after a short examination. "There are a few traces here of the same rubber composition I found on the waste. Can you tell me what it means?"

"Quite simple," Ned replied, as the boys gathered about him. "The use of rubber composition by men engaged in nefarious undertakings dates back to the time of the utilization of the whorls and lines of the human fingers as aids in the detection of crime."

"I guess I know what you are going to say," cried Frank.

"When the thumb- and finger-print experts got busy with their photographs and their enlarged reproductions, the criminals began studying on methods to offset this dangerous aid to detective work."

"I knew it," cried Frank.

"And so," Ned went on, "they conceived the idea of filling the lines on the fingers and hands and making them perfectly smooth. This is rubber paint," he went on. "The man who was hidden in here when we came in did not care to leave any finger marks behind him."

"But he did leave smooth blurs on the machines where his fingers touched them!" said Jack.

"Certainly, and so pointed out the location of his efforts. Still, I do not think he meditated disabling the Sea Lion. It is more probable that he believed Lieutenant Scott to be the expert in charge of the boat and sought to kill or disable him."

"See where the chump wiped his hands on waste," Jimmie cried.

Ned now made a still closer inspection of the room and was rewarded for his thoroughness by discovering a tiny pool of the rubber composition on the floor, close to the giant iron frame of the big dynamo. Looking at the pool through his glass he discovered bits of wool mixed with it. He put up his glass with a smile.

"We ought to be able to find this fellow now," he said, "if we get busy before he has time to change his clothes."

"Got him, have you?" asked Jack.

"I think I could pick him out of a thousand provided he is captured in the clothes he wore while here. His hand trembled while he was putting the rubber composition on his fingers and some of it dropped on his clothing and dripped off to the floor.

"There are shreds of blue wool in this composition on the floor—so you see he wore a blue woolen garment—probably a coat or pair of trousers. And, see here, the fellow lost all caution when he bounded out of the submarine, after extinguishing the lights, on my entrance.

"He had already wiped the rubber off his hands on the waste, and so his finger marks showed on the steel railing of the staircase. I'll just take a photo of them."

When this was accomplished, Ned and Jimmie drew the Sea Lion's boat to the edge of the float and launched it. Then, leaving Frank and Jack in charge of the submarine, with instructions to keep a close watch for suspicious characters, they turned the prow of the rowboat toward South Vallejo. The distance to the wharf was not great. In fact, the intruder seemed to have cleared it in a minute, either in a boat, which was improbable, or by swimming.

The Sea Lion lay off the United States Navy Yard, on the west of Mare Island, in the straits of the same name. The nearest landing place on the mainland, therefore, was South Vallejo.

It was after 8 o'clock when the boys reached the main street of the town and encountered a policeman in uniform. Ned at once asked for the office of the Coroner of Salano County.

"What's doing?" asked the policeman.

"I have business with him," Ned replied, not caring to create a sensation by reciting there in the street the details of what had taken place.

"Well," replied the policeman, "if you're so mighty close-mouthed regarding your business with the Coroner, you may find him yourself."

"All right," Ned replied. "I'll go to police headquarters. Perhaps the night desk man won't be so fresh."

"Say," growled the policeman, "you needn't get gay. I know my duty. So, if you don't mind, I'll take you to headquarters, saving you the trouble of asking for the place."

"I refuse to go with you," Ned replied.

"Oh, well," announced the other, "I'll take you along, just the same. I'm used to kids of your stamp. You're both under arrest, so you'd better come along without making any trouble."

As he spoke the policeman seized both boys roughly.

CHAPTER V

TWO WOLVES IN A PEN

"Take it quietly," Ned advised Jimmie, as the little fellow began struggling with the arm of the law. "We'll come out on top in the end, I take it."

"I'd like to knock the head off this fool cop!" Jimmie cried. "What right has he to go an' arrest us?"

"If it will take any load off your mind," the policeman replied, as the three waited on a corner for a patrol wagon, "I'll tell you what right I had to arrest you. There's a report at the office that a man who went into that submarine of yours never came out again."

"When was this report sent in?" asked Ned.

"Just a few moments ago," was the reply. "All the officers in the city are either watching for you or heading toward the boat. What have you done with Lieutenant Scott?"

"Who sent in the report?" asked Ned.

"I don't know his name, but the chief does. He says he went to the water front, on the island side, with the Lieutenant, that the Lieutenant went on board the Sea Lion with you and the others, and that he has not been seen since. What about it? Better confess and get an easy sentence."

"The officers who are on their way to the submarine will find out why the Lieutenant never came out," Ned said. "But about this man who made the report. Why was he waiting for Scott to leave the boat?"

"Said he had an understanding with him that he was to watch outside, as Scott did not exactly trust you New York kids. A little while ago he heard a commotion and calls for help on board, so he came up to report."

"Thank you for the information," Ned said. "Now, you can't get us to headquarters any too quickly."

"Where is Scott?" asked the officer.

"Dead," was the reply.

"Holy smoke!" cried the policeman. "Then I've arrested a couple of murderers!"

"If you'll hurry us to headquarters," Ned replied, "and the man who made this report is still there, I'll help you to arrest a real murderer. Here comes the wagon."

"Drive fast," ordered the policeman as the three entered the patrol wagon and the driver turned to inspect the boys. "I've got the fellows we're after," he added.

"Great luck!" the driver replied. "There'll be a big reward."

"Oh, I guess I know my business!" said the policeman, with a boastful chuckle.

The station was soon reached, and, without the least ceremony, the boys were pushed along to the cell block and locked up. Ned's demand that they be taken before the chief was not heeded.

"This is fine!" Jimmie said, from the next cell to the one occupied by Ned. "I like this."

Before Ned could reply, the chief of police made his appearance in the corridor outside, a great ring of keys in one hand. He unlocked the cell doors without speaking a word and motioned the boys out into the corridor.

Then, still without speaking, he pointed the way to his private office, ushered the lads in, closed and locked the door.

"Well?" he said, then.

"Will you send for the Coroner?" asked Ned.

"So Scott is dead?"

"Yes."

"Why did you kill him?"

Before opening his mouth to reply, Ned caught sight of a dark stain on the arm of the chair in which he was seated.

"Have you a microscope handy?" he asked.

The chief opened his eyes in amazement.

The question, coming at that time, seemed almost the raving of a mad man. This is the view the chief took of it, and he decided to conciliate the maniac.

"What do you want of a microscope?" he asked.

"I want to see if this spot is caused by the application of a certain rubber composition, and if there are shreds of blue wool mixed with it."

"I guess," the chief said, "that your proper place is the foolish house."

"While your men are bringing the microscope," Ned went on, coolly, "I want to ask you a few questions."

"Go ahead," laughed the chief, wondering what sort of insanity this was.

"Who sat in this chair last?" asked Ned.

"Why, the last visitor, of course."

"Can you now recall his name?"

"Curtis."

"How was he dressed?"

"In a blue suit."

"Where is he now?"

"I don't know. He said he would return as soon as the officers came back from the submarine."

"Yes he will!" Jimmie broke in.

"Does he belong here?" asked Ned.

The chief pointed to the west.

"Over in the navy yard," he said.

"So the blue suit he wore was a naval uniform?"

"Exactly."

The chief touched a bell on his desk and a policeman opened the door at the back of the room, connecting with the sergeant's room, and looked in.

"Get a microscope," the chief ordered, "and keep quiet about what is going on in here."

The sergeant nodded and went out.

"What did you say about that smear on the arm of the chair?" asked the chief, then.

He was beginning to understand that there was something besides mental trouble at the bottom of Ned's inquiries.

"I think," was the reply, "that an inspection of the spot will reveal a rubber composition used principally by the thieves of Paris as a paint to prevent palm and finger lines and whorls showing on things they take hold of."

The chief looked at the spot critically.

"Also, shreds from a blue uniform," Ned continued.

"We shall see," replied the chief.

The microscope was soon brought in, and then a close examination of the spot on the arm of the chair was made by the chief.

"What do you find?" asked Ned.

"I really can't say what it is," was the reply.

Ned took from a pocket a bit of the waste he had brought from the dynamo room of the submarine.

"Look at this," he said, "and see if the material in it appears to be the same as that on the chair. I mean, of course, the smudge on it."

The chief turned his instrument on the waste.

"It is the same," he declared, in a moment, "and I'd like to know where you got it."

"Do you find blue threads—well, not threads, exactly, but bits of fuzz—in the waste, too?"

"Yes, but the trace is faint."

"Well," Ned said, "the man who killed Lieutenant Scott is the man who gave you the information you speak of. He sat in this chair not long ago. I would advise a search for him."

"But he agreed to come back." "Of course he never will," Ned said. "Now, here is another point. You are going to have the Sea Lion searched?"

"Yes."

"Well, your men will find the body of Lieutenant Scott lying

G. Harvey Ralphson

on a couch there. In that case, they will doubtless arrest the two boys I left on watch there?"

"Certainly."

"And that will give the man who left this blur on the arm of this chair not long ago a chance to make off with the boat. I reckon you'll do well to look after that part of the case, for the submarine belongs to the Secret Service department of the Government, and Uncle Sam has use for it just at this time."

"The Secret Service department?" repeated the chief. "He said she was a scout boat Lieutenant Scott was going to coast south with."

"Did he say why he suspected that Lieutenant Scott was in danger?" asked Ned.

"He said you boys were suspicious characters who claimed to be able to operate a submarine, and that Scott was inclined to try you out."

Ned took a long envelope from a pocket of his coat and passed it, unopened, to the chief.

"Read the letter inside," he said, "and then get me to the Sea Lion as quickly as possible."

The chief opened the envelope and read the single sheet of typewritten paper it held.

"From the Secretary of the Navy!" he exclaimed.

"Exactly."

"I don't need to ask if you are the Ned Nestor mentioned in the letter, then. I saw a picture of you in a San Francisco newspaper, not long ago, and now recognize you as the boy referred to."

"Then take us to the submarine," urged Ned.

"It won't do no good to take us there after that cheap skate has geezled the boat," Jimmie cut in.

"And you are Jimmie," the chief went on. "I saw your picture, too. Well, this is quite a surprise for me," the chief added.

"You'll get a greater surprise if you let that murderer get off with the Sea Lion," Jimmie remarked.

The chief called the sergeant again and in a moment all was confusion in the police station. A wagon was called, and the chief and his ex- prisoners were soon on their way to the wharf, followed by the eyes of the policemen left behind.

"That's Ned Nestor, of New York," the boys heard one of the men on the iron steps in front saying as they passed, "and the little fellow is Jimmie McGraw. Great hit Preston made arresting them!"

But the minds of the boys were too full of anxiety regarding the fate of Scott and the Sea Lion to pay much attention to the words of flattery they overheard. If the unknown murderer succeeded in securing the arrest of Jack and Frank and getting away in the submarine, the whole trip would have to be abandoned, at least for the present.

Besides, Ned had no idea of going back to New York and reporting that he had been robbed of his boat under the very guns of the Mare Island Navy Yard. He urged the driver to make greater speed, and in a short time the wharf was in sight.

Half a dozen policemen were gathered about the end nearest the float which upheld the Sea Lion, and the figure of another showed at the top of the conning tower. As the police wagon dashed up to the wharf another rig came up on a run and halted close at the side of it.

"Hello," called the chief, recognizing a man on the seat, "how did you manage to get here so soon?"

"Some one 'phoned for me," was the hurried reply. "Where is the dead man?"

"In the submarine," answered an officer who had drawn closer to the official's buggy.

Without another word the newcomer leaped out and was conveyed to the Sea Lion in the rowboat Ned had left tied to the wharf.

"That's the Coroner," the chief said, in explanation. "He'll soon get at the bottom of this."

"Suppose we get aboard the Sea Lion," suggested Ned.

"Of course," said the chief, "you'll remain here a few days and assist in the capture of this fellow?"

"I shall have to ask for instructions from Washington," was the reply. "I really ought to get away on the steamer which sails in the morning."

When the three, using a boat an officer found nearby,

reached the main cabin of the Sea Lion they found Jack and Frank sitting by the table, handcuffed, repeating over and over again their individual and collective opinion of the police of Vallejo. Jimmie seemed to take great delight in taunting them.

"Black Bears in chains!" he roared.

"Huh, where have you Wolves been?" demanded Jack. "These cops said they had you in a pen!"

While the Coroner was making his examination the chief ordered the irons removed from the wrists of the boys. For a time the Coroner appeared to be puzzled. He lifted the hands of the apparently dead man and dropped them again. Then he held a pocket mirror before his lips.

"Look here," he said, presently, "I don't believe this man is dead."

"I hope you are right," Ned said, hopefully. "Still, the poison I got near killed me, while he must have gotten much more."

There was a short silence, during which the Coroner held his watch.

G. Harvey Ralphson

CHAPTER VI

NIGHT ON AN OCEAN FLOOR

"Over there, straight to the west," Ned said, pointing from the conning tower of the submarine, "is the coast of China, not far from seventy-five miles away."

"And there, to the north," Frank said, "lie the Taya Islands. The big fellow beyond is Hainan."

The sun was going down into the Gulf of Tong King like a ball of red fire, and the night was far from cool.

Jimmie declared he could hear the water hiss as the sun dipped its red rim under the waves. The boy now stood by Ned's side, looking over the wonderful scene.

"We've been somewhere near here before," he said. "You remember the time we came over to this side of the world and found a key to a treaty box? Well, we wasn't far from this spot at one time."

"Right you are," Frank replied. "Only we hope to find something more important than a key now. I hope they've had use for a cell key in connection with that mix-up at Mare Island Navy Yard."

"It was rotten to let that fellow get away!" Jimmie declared. "I just knew they would."

"We were all so astonished at the recovery of Lieutenant Scott," Ned observed, "that we overlooked a few things we ought to have kept in mind. Wasn't it glorious! Think of Scott coming out of it all right at last!"

"Well, he said he was a fixture on the coast until he found the man who came so near killing him," Frank said, in a moment, "and I hope he'll make good."

"Huh," Jimmie interrupted, "if you think that fellow is on the Pacific coast yet, you've got another think comin'. You remember the Diver left San Francisco just about the time we did."

"What has that to do with it?"

"Most nothin' at all, only he sailed in her."

"You're a wise little man!"

"And, what's more, we'll see the Diver come pluggin' along here before we get this job done," Jimmie went on. "That Captain Moore and his son are out for blood."

"But the Diver will require at least a couple of months to get here," urged Frank. "We can get away before that time."

"You don't know what the Moores will do," Ned said. "I rather agree with Jimmie, that we shall see something of the Diver before we leave this part of the world."

"I hope so," Frank said.

"Well, who's for the bottom of the sea?" demanded Jimmie. "I want to see what's down there before the Bogy Man gets me."

"I don't mind going down," Ned said. "Come on, we'll close the top hatch and drop to the bottom, then, if conditions are right, we'll enter the water closet, put on the diving suits, and take a walk on the floor of the big water."

"Suppose we all go," suggested Frank.

"Perhaps it may be well for two to remain aboard in order to help the others out, if necessary," Ned observed.

"All right," Frank said. "Catch a fish by the tail and bring him in for supper."

"To-morrow," Jimmie said, "you can take a run on the riparian rights an' chase whales."

"I'll wait and see whether you boys come out alive," laughed Frank. "I'm a little leary about mixing with the funny little fishes. Some of 'em may bite!"

After a thoroughly interesting voyage, the boys had at last reached the scene of their labors. It was now the 2oth of October. The Sea Lion had rode securely on the float, and Ned and his companions had spent most of the time during the journey under the great hood which covered the submarine, studying the mechanism and making themselves thoroughly familiar with the big machine.

Arriving off the Taya Islands, the float had been submerged by opening the sluiceways and filling the tanks with water. The Sea Lion behaved admirably when she came to the surface after cutting away from the companion of her voyage.

As there were no appliances for lifting the big float, she was now at the bottom of the sea for all time, unless broken away from the water- filled tanks by divers, in which case the upper works would come to the surface. It was with feelings of keen regret that the boys saw the great barge, as it might well be called, lying, deserted, on the ocean floor.

As has been shown by the conversation between the boys in the conning tower, Lieutenant Scott had fully recovered from the effects of the poisonous fumes he had inhaled in the submarine on the night of Ned's arrest at South Vallejo. Physicians stated at the time that his recovery was due to the fact that the conning tower hatch was open when the deadly gas was released. Ned, it was also stated, would have been dead in a few moments if the hatch had been closed.

Search had been made, both by the police and the naval detectives, for the author of the mischief, but he had not been found. It was believed that his purpose in reporting the result of his own deviltry to the chief of police was to secure the arrest of the boys on the Sea Lion and make off with her.

Ned did not say so, when discussing the matter with the officers, but he was satisfied that the Moores were at the bottom of the trouble. The Captain had resigned, and had been observed lounging about the wharf in New York where the Sea Lion lay, and had, it was afterwards learned, been seen in San Francisco on the day before the arrival of Lieutenant Scott and the Boy Scouts.

In reaching this conclusion Ned assigned envy as the prime motive on the part of the Captain and his son. They had expected to be assigned the duty of searching the ocean floor for the wreck of the mail steamer. In their great disappointment nothing was more probable than that they had resolved to hamper the efforts of their successful rivals in every way.

But there was still another view of the case which might be considered. The gold in the hull of the wrecked steamer would become the spoil of the first submarine to reach her.

With the double incentive, greed joined to a thirst for revenge, it would not be at all strange if the Moores had risked everything in their efforts to prevent the Sea Lion leaving the Navy Yard on her long trip. It was Ned's private opinion, too, that the son had been the one to sneak into the submarine and attack the Lieutenant with the poisonous gas.

Leaving Frank and Jack in the machine room, Ned and Jimmie entered the water chamber and closed the door, which, however, was provided with a plate glass panel of great thickness, so that light from the other room supplied plenty of illumination.

It was not designed to submerge the Sea Lion until the boys were all ready to step out. Four deep-sea suits hung on hooks in the water chamber, one for each of the boys.

These suits were not much different from those usually worn by deep-sea divers. They were of seamless rubber composition, braced across the breast with bars of steel in order to offset the great pressure of the lower levels and give the lungs plenty of room for expansion.

The helmets, which fitted on the neck of the suits, were lighter than those in ordinary use, but fully as strong. The cords attached to the helmets were very long, and the air-hose admitted of a range of at least three hundred feet.

By the side of each suit lay an electric searchlight of special construction and a long steel pole, shaped something like a crowbar, but very slender and strong. This latter for defense in case attack should be made by some monster of the deep.

"Say," Jimmie grinned, slipping on his suit, "these spring suits look to me like someone to button us up in the back."

"I don't see where you find buttons," replied Ned.

"Look here, then!"

The boy pointed to the screws designed to secure the helmets.

"You button me up, and I'll button you up," Ned laughed. "We've got to learn to do such things."

"I'll catch a shark an' get him to learn how," cried Jimmie. "I wonder how I would look in this suit walkin' down the Bowery. Gee! I bet the boys would jump out of their skins if they saw me comin'. They'd think their master had come to claim 'em!"

The boys worked industriously for a time, settling themselves in the rather clumsy suits, and then all was ready save putting on the heavy helmets. Jimmie pointed to a belt about the waist of his suit.

"What's that for?" he asked, pulling at a hook which was suspended from the steel circlet.

"That's to hang your searchlight on," was the reply. "There may come a time when you'll want both hands to operate that spike thing you've got to carry."

At last the helmets were adjusted, the cords and air-hose attached, and then Ned motioned to the boys, watching with grinning eyes through the plate glass panel, to turn on the air. The first sensation on receiving the air was one of exhilaration, but this soon passed off.

Ned saw, by looking through the immense goggles which Jimmie wore, that the lad was almost bursting with laughter, but he knew that this effect would soon pass away. He pushed a button, and signaled to Frank to fill the water tanks.

As the water chamber filled the boys felt a cold circle rise from their toes to their heads. They felt a sinking motion, and soon the mysterious life of the ocean became visible through the outer glass door of the water chamber.

The Sea Lion dropped evenly to the bottom. The supply of air was as perfect as it could well be. When the faint jar told Ned that the submarine was at last resting on the bed of the tropical sea he released a heavy bar which held the door, pushed it back against considerable pressure, and stepped out.

Jimmie followed, and Ned stopped long enough to point to the lines as a warning that they should not be allowed to become tangled, and struck off. It was early in the evening, and there was a moon, almost at the full.

The depth at that point was not great, scarcely more than sixty feet. The pressure of the water overhead made walking rather difficult, and the boys were strange to the lines they were drawing after them, but they made good progress until they came to the end of the air-hose.

It was not as dark under the waves as might have been expected. The light of the sun penetrates, ordinarily, to a depth of not far from forty feet, and the moon's rays on this night were very strong. It was not light enough for the boys to see objects around them, but there was a soft illumination above their heads not dissimilar to the faint haze of light which lies over a country landscape situated at no great distance from a city bright with electricity.

By using the searchlights, however, the boys were able to distinguish objects directly about them. They were on a level plain of pure white sand. Ages and ages ago this pavement laid so smoothly on the ocean floor had existed in the form of rocks.

Through countless years it had faced the assaults of the waves, until at last, in utter defeat, it had succumbed to the mighty force and dropped in fine grains to the lower levels of the world. It seemed to Ned that it had lain there for centuries, with never a storm to pile it into ridges or break its level surface into pits.

The scene about the boys was indescribably beautiful. The inhabitants of the sea rivaled the rainbow in brilliancy of coloring. There were more forms of life in sight than either of the boys had ever imagined in existence.

Queer-shaped sea creatures with long tails darted about the rubber-clad figures, and now and then an inquisitive fish with curious eyes poked its nose against the eye plates, as if intent on discovering what sort of creature it was that carried a sunrise in its head.

There were monster creatures in sight, too, and Jimmie jabbed at one of them and brought blood. This brought others, and in a short time the boys found themselves surrounded by a school of sharks.

Ned threw himself down on the sandy bottom and motioned to Jimmie to do likewise. This seemed to surprise the sharks, for they nosed around for only a moment longer. Seeing no opportunity of getting under their prospective dinners, they switched their tails angrily, like a cat in a temper, and swam off about their business, if they had any.

G. Harvey Ralphson

But Ned had little interest in the sea life about him. At another time, and under other conditions, he would have enjoyed the novelty of the scene to the fullest, but now he was anxiously watching for some indication of the presence of the wreck of the Cutaria.

He was as certain as it was possible to be that the Sea Lion had descended almost at the exact spot where the ill-fated vessel went down. The hull should be out there in the sand somewhere, and he lost no time in making his investigations.

But there was nothing on the smooth surface to show that any vessel had ever rested there. Away to the north, however, the boy finally saw what looked like an elevation.

His flashlight, however, would not throw its beams to the point of interest, and he decided to return to the Sea Lion, rest for the remainder of the night, and shift the submarine in the morning.

Motioning to his companion, therefore, he turned toward the door to the water chamber. They had proceeded only a few steps when something seemed to pass over their heads.

It was as if a heavy cloud had drifted over a summer sky, outlining its shape on the fields below for an instant and then passing on. Jimmie caught Ned's arm and pointed upward.

It was plain that the little fellow had caught sight of something his companion had missed, but of course he could not explain then and there what it was. Ned hastened his steps, and soon stood at the door of the water chamber, which had been left open.

As Jimmie pushed into the water-filled apartment by his side and Ned was about to close the door and expel the water from the chamber, as well as from the tanks of the submarine, something which flashed like polished steel hurtled through the water and struck the bottom just outside the doorway.

Ned stepped out and picked it up. It was a keen-edge knife, such as sailors carry. On the handle was a single initial—"D."

Ned knew what that meant. Through some strange agency, by means of some unaccountable assistance, the Diver had reached the scene of the proposed operations of the Sea Lion.

From this time on, it would be a battle of wits—perhaps worse!

CHAPTER VII

THE SECRET OF THE HOLD

In response to Ned's hand on the lever, the water door closed and the pumps in the next compartment soon cleared not only the sea vestibule but the tanks of the submarine of seawater.

In a moment the Sea Lion lifted to the surface, and Ned lost no time in relieving himself of his helmet. Then, still attired in the rubber suit, he hastened to the conning tower, where he found Jack, glass in hand, sweeping the moonlit sea eagerly. There was a faint haze off to the west, but nothing more. Whatever had passed above the submerged boat, on the surface, had wholly disappeared, though the time had been very short.

"What did you see?"

Ned asked the question because Jack's manner indicated excitement, if not anxiety.

"Just a shadow," was the reply.

"It might have been a shadow, passing over the moon, the shadow of a cloud, or a cloud itself," suggested Frank, sticking his head out of the hatchway.

Ned pointed to the sky. There was not a cloud in sight.

"It must have been something of the kind," Jack mused, "for no boat could get out of sight so soon."

"Not even a submarine?" asked Ned.

"What do you mean by that?"

"Did you see a submarine?"

Both questions were asked in a breath.

"No," replied Ned, "I did not see a submarine, but I don't believe any cloud passing over the sky would drop anything like this."

He passed the knife to Jack and took the glass. Jack opened his eyes wide as he examined the weapon and noted the initial on the handle. He turned impulsively to Ned.

"Where did you get it?" he asked.

"At the bottom."

"Did you find it lying there?"

"It fell just as I reached the water chamber."

"Then how the dickens did the Diver get away so soon?" demanded the boy.

"It sure did fall from the Diver," agreed Frank, taking the knife and examining it.

"It would seem so," Ned replied, "but, of course, the initial may be merely a coincidence."

"I guess we're in for it."

"But how did the Diver get here so soon after our arrival?" asked one of the boys.

Ned looked grave for a moment, and then replied, his manner showing how fully he appreciated the importance of his words:

"What I fear is that she got here first."

"And found the wreck?"

"She might have done so."

"Did you see anything of the Cutaria down there?" asked Frank.

"Not a bloomin' thing," answered Jimmie, making his appearance on the conning tower.

"The Diver might have towed it away," suggested Jack.

"Impossible!" cried the others, in chorus.

"Anyway," Jack continued, "we're up against the real goods now. If the Diver is here we'll have a scrap."

"But suppose it should be some other outfit?" asked Frank. "Some pirate outfit after the gold?"

"Still there would be a scrap."

"That's one advantage of goin' with Ned," Jimmie edged in. "You most always get into a scrap!"

"Well," Ned said, presently, "we may as well drop down and keep our lights low. If the Diver is here, the Moores are aware of our presence, and we must be prepared for anything."

In ten minutes the submarine lay at the bottom of the sea, with no lights showing, every plate glass window having been shuttered on the outside by a system of protection which was one of the best features of the craft. Then Ned explained that he had seen, at some distance, an apparent elevation rising from the sand.

"That may be the wreck," he said.

"I move we go and see," shouted Jimmie.

"In the darkness?" asked Frank.

"It is as light out there now," Jack declared, "as it will ever be, unless some subterranean volcano lights up and makes fireworks on the bottom, so we may as well be off."

"All right," Ned said, in a moment. "I was meditating a little rest to-night, but it may be advisable to get to work at once. For all we know the Moores may be stripping the wreck, even now."

"What I can't understand," Jack said, sticking to the first proposition, "is how the Diver got here in such good time."

"As has been said, it may be some other craft," Frank consoled.

"Don't believe it," insisted Jimmie. "The boat that dropped that knife is a submarine, else how could she disappear so suddenly? She may be watching us now."

"Or her divers may be prowling around the Sea Lion!" Jack created a little sensation by saying.

"What would be the use of prowling around outside the boat?" asked Jimmie. "They couldn't hear anything, or see anything."

"But a torpedo will act under water," suggested Frank. "Those chaps are equal to anything."

"Shall we go out and look around?" asked Jack.

Ned hesitated. He really was alarmed at the situation. He knew how desperate the Moores must be, and he had no doubt that in some strange way the Diver had been brought to the scene of the wreck.

"If you and Frank are partial to a moonlight stroll under sixty feet of water," he finally said, "you may as well put on your water suits and look around."

"Leave Jimmie here to watch the boat and come with us," urged Jack.

"Go on," Jimmie advised. "I can run this shebang, all right. Go on and see what you can see."

"If we are going out to-night," Ned said, after reflection, "we may as well shift the Sea Lion and inspect the bottom over where we saw the apparent elevation."

"Yes; that may be the wreck," Jack admitted.

So the submarine was moved a short distance to the north, about the space which had seemed to separate the boys from the elevation, and preparations were made for going out. Jimmie was rather pleased at the idea of being left in charge of the submarine.

"Of course you'll not touch the machinery," Ned warned. "All you can do is to see that the air pumps are kept going. Any motion of the boat, you understand, might break or disarrange the hose carrying the air to us, so be careful."

"Oh, I guess I don't want to murder any of you," laughed the little fellow. "Go ahead and I'll run things all right on board the boat. I could operate her anywhere."

The Sea Lion was lifted only a trifle in order to make the change to the new location. As she moved along she was not much more than a fathom from the level sand below.

This was done by regulating the water in the tanks to the pressure at the depth it was desired to navigate. The delicate mechanisms designed to show depth, pressure, air value, and all the important details of a submarine were absolutely perfect.

So the three boys entered the water chamber, leaving Jimmie grinning through the glass panel. When the boat was brought to the bottom they opened the outer door and stepped out.

The Sea Lion had traversed only a short distance, yet the surface upon which the lads walked seemed very different from the smooth sand level Ned had seen before. There were now little ridges of sand, and now and then a pit opened up almost under their feet.

A dozen yards from where they emerged from the submarine

they came upon the elevation which Ned had observed on his first trip out. It was not, however, a submerged rock or a bit of harder soil in the desert of sand. It was the hull of a wrecked vessel.

Ned moved along one side of the wreck, as far as his air-hose would permit him to go, and was satisfied that he had found the lost mail ship. The sand was already drifting against her sides, but she was still far from buried.

On the port side, about a third of the way to the stern from the bow, the boy discovered the wound which had brought the stately vessel to her present position. She lay, tilted about a quarter, in eighty feet of water.

Ned wondered why passing vessels had not discovered her. The tall stacks had been beaten down, probably snapped off at the collision, but the superstructure was high, and not far below the surface, Ned thought.

After motioning Jack and Frank to remain at the break in the side of the ship, Ned clambered up and, being careful to protect his air-hose and line from the jagged edges of the wound, crept inside. His electric flashlight revealed the interior only a short distance ahead of him, but at the very outset he saw that some of the air-tight compartments remained intact.

There was a lifting, swaying motion occasionally which told him that there was still air imprisoned in the broken ship. At that distance from the surface there would be no wave motion to produce the oscillations he observed.

"It is very strange," he mused, as he clambered over bales, chests and boxes in the hold, "that the ship should have gone down so quickly. Telegraphic reports at the time of the accident—if it was an accident—stated that she sank slowly. It would require only a little assistance to bring her to the surface."

The boy made his way as far into the interior as he could with his comparatively short air-hose, and then turned back to where he had left Jack and Frank. He had found it impossible, on account of the shifting to the prow of the hold cargo, to reach the cabin and the captain's offices without entering from the top deck.

As he turned around he stopped an instant, his attention attracted by a sound which seemed to come from beyond the bulkhead back of him. It sounded almost like the hiss of escaping steam. The lad knew that it must be a strong vibration which could thus make itself felt at that distance below the surface and through the heavy helmet he wore.

The more he considered the matter the clearer became the fact that it was actually uniform sound he heard. That is, sound brought to his ears by the water.

Some force might be moving the water, and the motion might be conveying to his ears, through the thin sides of the air-hose, the story of the action of the waves, if waves could be created at that depth.

As he listened to the steady beating he became convinced that some unknown power was at work in the wreck. What it was he could not even guess.

Then he heard sharper sounds which seemed to be created by steel striking steel. The jar brought the sound waves to his ears quite distinctly.

"Either I'm going daffy," the boy mused, "or there is some

G. Harvey Ralphson

one at work on the wreck."

He left the hold and, without giving the others to understand that he had discovered anything of importance, began an examination of the sand along the line of the bottom. His air-hose was not long enough to admit of passing entirely around the vessel, so he motioned to the boys to accompany him and turned back to the submarine.

"Did you hear anything down there?" asked he as soon as the helmets had been removed.

"What are you talking about?" asked Frank, with a laugh. "Water would not convey sound to the ear."

"But the jar of water would," observed Jack. "I heard a jar while I was down there."

"I don't believe it!" Jimmie cut in.

"When in swimming," said Frank, "did you ever sit on the bottom of the swimming hole and pound two stones together?"

"Of course," laughed the little fellow.

"And you heard a noise?"

"I believe I did, but it was not such a noise as one would hear from the same cause in the air."

"Well," Ned went on, "I heard noises down there, too, and I'll tell you right here that I'm alarmed."

"Scared!" roared Jimmie.

"Alarmed at what?" demanded Frank. "I didn't see anything to be alarmed at."

"I have no theory as to what it was I heard," Ned went on, "but I'm going to get a longer air-hose, shift the Sea Lion so she will hang over the wreck, and go down again right away."

"I'm ready!" laughed Jack. "I want to hear that noise again."

"Do you think there are men down there removing the gold?" asked Jack.

CHAPTER VIII

ON GUARD UNDER THE SEA

"If there is anybody at work on the wreck," Ned replied, "they may be removing the gold or they may be searching the vessel for incriminating documents."

"I guess any documents found down there will be pretty wet," laughed Jack.

"They may be in sealed boxes," Ned replied. "Anyway, if there are important documents on board they might be rendered legible by proper and judicious handling." "Here we go, then," Jack exclaimed. "I'll expel the water in the tanks until the Sea Lion rests at the right altitude, over the wreck, and we can enter by way of the decks."

"But what will the other fellows be doing while we are getting into position?" asked Frank.

"Gettin' ready to cut our lines, probably," interposed Jimmie.

"That's a fact," Jack said. "If there are men working in the ship they must be supplied with air by a submarine. How could that be done, I'd like to know."

"They might anchor the submarine some distance away," replied Ned, "and lay an air-hose along the bottom. If attached to the hose leading into the helmets before being placed, two or three might work from such a supply, and such a system, too, would obviate a good deal of the danger to be feared from crossed lines."

"You've got it all figured out!" cried Jimmie.

"Well," Frank intervened, "I'll bet that he has it right. Those Moore persons were not born yesterday."

"That's right," Jack admitted. "We saw enough of the Captain in the Black Bear club-room in New York to know that he is an expert in the submarine business. He may be an imitation fop and a bounder, as he would say, but he certainly is next to his job."

"Why wouldn't it be a good idea to sneak around in our water suits until we find the lines an' cut them?" asked Jimmie.

"That would be plain murder," Ned replied.

"I guess they wouldn't hesitate long if the conditions were reversed," Frank suggested, "still, I wouldn't like to be in with anything as brutal as that."

"Come to think of it," Jimmie admitted, "I wouldn't, either."

"I don't get the idea of these incriminating documents," Jack said, in a moment. "That is one thing I did not pay attention to in the talk with Captain Moore at the clubroom."

"What he said was this," Ned explained. "The Government is accused, in certain hostile foreign circles, of conspiring with the leaders of the revolution now brewing in China. He

G. Harvey Ralphson

declared that the Washington officials were even charged with sending the gold to the rebels by the roundabout way of the present Chinese Government."

"You'll have to come again!" laughed Frank. "I'm dense as to that part of it. It is too subtle for me."

"Me, too," Jimmie asserted.

"All I know about it," Ned answered, "is that Captain Moore declared that the rebel leaders were purposely posted as to the shipment of the gold, and that they were to seize it as soon as it left the protection of the American flag, if they could. At least they were to be given a chance to do so."

"Even in that case," Frank reasoned, "the Washington people wouldn't be foolish enough to place incriminating papers with the shipment. The whole scheme might fail, you know."

"It does look pretty fishy," Ned remarked, "but the ways of diplomacy are often crooked ways. Anyway, it is claimed by some that the mail boat was rammed, that it was no accident that sent her to keep company with McGinty at the bottom of the sea."

Jack expelled the water from the tanks of the Sea Lion until the instruments in the machine room showed her to be near the surface, and, as Ned estimated, directly above the wreck. Then an anchor was sent out, to prevent any possible drifting, and Ned, Frank and Jack put on their helmets again.

The lines used for signaling and the air-hose had both been spliced, and it was figured that any part of the wreck could now be visited. The drop lines were also longer, and the machinery for hauling the divers up on signal was made ready for use.

"We can't walk out and in the Sea Lion now," Ned said, "and a good deal depends on the vigilance of the boy left in the boat. Watch for the slightest signal, Jimmie," he warned.

The touching of a lever unwound the lifting and lowering lines when all was ready, and in a minute the three boys found themselves on the upper deck of the wreck. It was tilted at an angle of about twenty degrees, so great care was exercised in traversing it.

As Jimmie swung the lever which lowered the three boys he peered out of a darkened window. He saw only the dim surface light.

"They've got sense enough not to show any light," he mused, "so the thieves won't know what is going on unless they see the shadow overhead, or run into one of the fellows."

Leaving Frank, as the most cautious of the boys, to guard the lines and air-hose when they touched sharp angles, Ned, accompanied by Jack, advanced down the main companion-way and was soon in the large and handsomely furnished cabin.

Then the electric searchlights were put to use, and the great apartment lay partly exposed to view. Their entrance into the room seemed to create something like a current in the water, and articles of light weight came driving at them.

Ned turned sick and faint as a dead body lifted from the floor and a ghastly face was turned toward his own. A few unfortunate ones had gone down with the ship, and most of the bodies lay in this cabin.

Those who had remained on deck until the final plunge had, of course, drifted away. However, the boy soon recovered his equilibrium, and went about his work courageously, notwithstanding the fact that many terrifying forms of marine life swam and squirmed around him.

Clinging to heavy tables and chairs to prevent slipping, the boys made their way to that part of the ship where, according to their drawings, the captain's cabin had been. Their first duty was to make search for any sealed papers which might be there.

The room was located at last, and then Ned motioned to Jack to extinguish his light. The boy obeyed orders with a feeling of dread.

It was dark as the bottomless pit in the cabin now, and fishes and squirming things brushed against his legs and rubbed against the line which was supplying him with air.

In all the experiences of the Boy Scouts nothing like this had ever been encountered before. In Mexico, in the Philippines, in the Great Northwest, in the Canal Zone, in the cold air far above the roof of the world, they had usually been in touch with all the great facts of Nature, but now they seemed separated from all mankind—buried in a fathomless pit filled with unclean things.

The door of the captain's cabin was closed. Ned put his ear against it, then reached out and took Jack by the arm. The latter understood the order and crowded close.

From the other side came sharp blows, and through the key-hole came the glow of illuminated water. Ned's worst fears were realized. Some one had reached the wreck in advance of his party.

He knew that he could not justly be censured for the activity of his enemies, and yet the thought that he was in danger of failing in his mission brought the hot blood surging to his head. He did not stop at that time to deliberate as to how the hostile forces had gained this advantage in time.

He did not even try to solve the problem as to the personality of the hostile element. The men working on the other side of the door to the captain's cabin might have crossed the Pacific in the Diver, or they might have been recruited from foreign seaports.

The question did not particularly interest him. The point with him was that they were there.

And, now, what course ought he to pursue? For a time, as he stood against the door, he could reach no conclusion.

Directly, however, the important question presented by the unusual situation came to the boy's mind. It was this:

Where was the boat into which the workers on the other side of the door proposed to remove the plunder?

The Diver, or some other efficient submarine must be close at hand. The men who were searching the captain's room were being supplied with air from some source.

And here was another question:

Had the gold already been removed?

It seemed to Ned that the first thing for him to do was to locate the submarine. For all he knew, prowlers from her might be nosing around the Sea Lion.

He had left the door to the water chamber open, of course,

G. Harvey Ralphson

and so it must remain until he returned. Jimmie, owing to a defect afterwards corrected, could not expel the water while the door was open, nor could he close the door from the interior.

Fearful that some mischief was on foot, he grasped Jack by the arm and hastened back to where Frank had been left. His first care should be to find the exact location of the hostile submarine and then see that no air-hose reached from her to the Sea Lion.

The three boys passed out of the wreck and came to the stern of the once fine ship. She had gone down prow first, and the stern was a little above the level sand floor of the sea.

Instead of passing around the stern and coming out on the other side, the boys halted and crouched down, so as to see under the keel. As the outer shell of the ship was here at least a yard above the bottom, it was plain that the cargo had swept forward when she went down, thus holding her by the nose.

There was no longer any doubt as to what was going on. There, only a few yards away, lay the dark bulk of a submarine. Only for a light glimmering through the closed door of the water chamber it could not have been seen at all.

The men who were working in the wreck had taken no chances in leaving the boat. Their lines and air-hose passed through the outer door in well-guarded openings, and the interior was as safe from intrusion as a walled-in fortress.

Ned regretted that he had not observed the same precaution in leaving the Sea Lion, still he did not believe that his boat had been attacked. After a few moments devoted to observation, Ned crept around the keel and looked down the side of the ship which lay toward the submarine. Men with electric lamps in their helmets were working there.

They appeared to be forcing an entrance into the lower hold of the ship through a small break in the shell. This led him to the conclusion that the way to the very bottom was blocked from the inside, and that the gold—if it had been stored there—had not yet been removed.

He returned to his chums and all three started back to the Sea Lion. The men about the wreck were all so busy that it did not seem to Ned that they knew of the presence there of his submarine.

Still, he searched the bottom, as he passed along, with both hands and feet for any line which, leaving the stranger, might be leading to her rival. Finally he discovered, much to his annoyance, a hauling line and an air-hose leading in the direction he was going.

"I'm afraid," he thought, "that Jimmie is in trouble."

G. Harvey Ralphson

CHAPTER IX

"JIMMIE'S FOOLISH—LIKE A FOX"

Left alone in the Sea Lion, Jimmie spent most of his time watching from a darkened window. He could distinguish little in the faint sifting of moonlight which dropped down from the sparkling surface of the sea, but there was companionship even in that.

He had been instructed by Ned to keep the interior dark, and so he watched the ocean floor for the lights which his chums might be obliged to turn on. As the reader knows, however, the exploring party showed no lights at all until the interior of the wreck had been gained.

Listening and waiting, half inclined to admit that he was just a little bit lonesome, the boy stood at his post for about a quarter of an hour. Then he saw an opaque object moving toward the submarine.

It was not a shark or other monster of the sea, for it walked upright and seemed to move up and down as it came to the little undulations in the ocean floor. When it came nearer Jimmie moved toward the door of the water chamber.

"That must be Ned," he thought, "comin' back alone. Now, I

wonder if anythin' has happened to Frank an' Jack?"

For a moment the heart of the lad throbbed wildly, then he calmed himself with the thought that in case of accident he would have been notified by the lifting lines. The air machine was working perfectly, too, and this indicated that all was well below.

Finally the moving object came to a position about ten yards distant from the submarine and stopped. He was now about fifty feet below the window out of which Jimmie looked, for the Sea Lion, as has been said, lay well up from the bottom, not exactly over the wreck but not far from it.

In a moment the boy saw the glimmer of a lamp down where the man was, and saw that it was moving about on the bottom. Lights, of course, do not show in water as they do in air, and so it was only a faint illumination that Jimmie observed.

Still, he could see that whoever was carrying the light was fumbling about on the bottom. He watched intently for a moment and then saw the man coming toward him, swimming straight up.

"I guess it's one of the boys," Jimmie mused. "He must have lost his line, and when I saw him fumbling he must have been removing the weights designed to hold him down in spite of the air in the helmet."

This appeared to be a good explanation, and the boy stood with his face pressed against the glass panel of the water chamber door, waiting for whoever it was to enter, close the apartment, and push the lever that controlled the exhaust which emptied the chamber.

At last the swimmer clambered into the chamber, and the waiting boy was about to switch on a light when a suspicious action on the part of the other caused him to hesitate. He could observe the actions of the man in the water on the other side of the glass panel quite clearly now, and was alarmed at what he saw him doing.

Instead of drawing his air-hose in with him and coiling it carefully so as to clear the doorway and still leave free passage for the air which was being pumped into it, he laid the hose carefully in a slide- covered groove in the edge of the door. The hose did not seem to be quite large enough to fill the groove, and the fellow took something soft and pliable from a pocket and wrapped around it.

Then he closed the door and pushed the lever which released the power that forced the water out of the chamber. Only one inference was to be drawn from the scene which Jimmie had witnessed.

The man in the water chamber was a stranger. This was merely an attempt to get possession of the Sea Lion.

The fellow was breathing air pumped into his hose by some other boat than the Sea Lion. He had cast off his weights in order to gain the chamber, which neither one of the boys would have found necessary, as they would have been carried up by the machinery which worked the lifting and descending lines.

Another thing the boy realized, as he waited with anxiety for the next move. The man, whoever he was, was thoroughly familiar with the plan of the Sea Lion.

The grooves in the edge of the door had been planned so as to give entrance to visitors who were not receiving their air from the Sea Lion. No one was believed to know anything about this arrangement—no one save the builders and the Secret Service men.

While Jimmie watched, the intruder moved the lever and the water in the chamber began to lower. When the water was forced out fresh air was automatically forced in.

Before long the intruder disconnected his hose with his helmet and threw the end over a hook provided for that purpose. When the water was all out he knocked heavily on the door leading to the room where Jimmie stood.

"There'll be doings here directly," the boy thought.

Again and again the visitor beat upon the door, but Jimmie gave no sign. He could not well observe the man now, for, with the water out of the chamber, the light carried by the man inside shone brightly against the glass panel, and the boy would have been observed had he stood close to it.

Jimmie grew more anxious as the seconds passed. He was trying to put away the thought that the intruder had cut the air-hose attached to the helmets of his friends.

For all he knew all three boys might be lying drowned, on the floor of the ocean. The thought was unbearable, and he resolved to banish it in action.

His first impulse was to disconnect the exhaust and fill the chamber with water. The man in there had disconnected his air-hose and would soon drown.

But the brutality of such a course soon presented itself, and Jimmie cast about for some other method of meeting the dangerous situation. He could hear the visitor fumbling at the

G. Harvey Ralphson

door, and wondered if he knew the secret of opening it.

After a time it seemed to the listening boy that the fellow was feeling in the right locality for the hidden spring which would open the door from the other side, and sprang for the bar which secured it against such entrance. Then he dropped the bar and stood wiping the sweat from his forehead.

"If I bar the door," he mused, "that robber will cut the air-hose protecting the boys outside, if he has not already done so. I've just got to let him in here an' take chances."

He hastened to the back of the room and brought a long coil of rope. Making a running noose in one end, he released several loops from the big coil and held them loosely in his hand.

"I wonder if I can assist him into our princely apartments?" thought the boy, whimsically. "If I can get this rope around his body and over his arms, I'll be the boss of the precinct! I expect he'll tumble around a good deal, but I guess I can quell him!"

The boy waited in the darkness until a faint click told him that the intruder had discovered the spring. This was followed by a slam as the sliding door fell back.

Then all was still. Jimmie, hidden in the shadows, prepared to throw his lasso as soon as the visitor left the doorway.

"Hello!"

The voice carried a hoarse challenge.

"Any one here?"

The man was still in the doorway, and was swinging his light about so as to give him a better view of the room.

"If he would only drop his arms!" Jimmie mused. "I'd like to hit him with a ballclub!"

Directly the fellow did drop his arms, and at the same moment stepped out of the shelter of the doorway. This was what Jimmie had been waiting for, and he lost no time in acting.

The rope cut the air and descended over the intruder's head and arms. The lad's hours of practice while playing cowboy now proved to be of great worth.

Jimmie gave a quick jerk as the rope landed and he ran to the back of the room. He heard the other fall, and knew by the weight that he was dragging him.

When he gained the wall he switched on the light and reached to a shelf for a weapon. When he faced his captive he held an automatic revolver in his hand.

By this time a torrent of expletives was coming through the helmet opening where the air-hose had entered. The prisoner rolled about on the floor, trying to get to his feet.

"Whoo-pee!" shouted the boy. "Look what one can catch out of the ocean!"

A roar of rage was the only answer.

"Take off that helmet!" commanded the boy.

A muffled challenge came from the interior.

"All right," said the boy, "then I'll take it off for you. But I'll have this gun handy, and if you try any foolishness you won't hold water when I get done shootin'."

Before long the helmet was off, and Jimmie was looking into as evil a face as he had ever seen. It was the face of a stranger, and yet there seemed something familiar about it.

"What sort of a game is this?" demanded the captive. "If you know what's good for you, you'll quit this cowboy business."

"Who are you?" asked Jimmie.

A snarl was the only reply. The enraged man was tugging fiercely at the rope.

"Quit it!" warned Jimmie. "I'll have to put you to sleep if you try that."

"You don't dare!"

"Don't four-flush!" the boy advised.

"Release me!"

Jimmie sat down and leveled the weapon at the struggling man.

"I guess I'd better shoot," he said, calmly. "I suppose you've cut the boys' air-hose, and I'll have to get back to New York the best way I can—alone. So, you see, I can't be bothered with you."

The captive ceased his struggles and managed to rise to a sitting position. His eyes were not so threatening as before.

"No," he declared, "I didn't cut the hose."

"Why? You're equal to such a trick."

"I was told not to."

Jimmie hesitated a moment. He wished devoutly that he could believe what the fellow said.

"Who told you not to?" he then asked.

The captive shook his head.

"I don't know his name," he said.

"And you are sailing with him?"

"All I know is that he is called the Captain."

"I see," said the boy. "Now, how comes it that you know so much of the plans of the Sea Lion?"

"What makes you think I do?"

"You found the groove in the door, and also the spring that opens the door to the water chamber."

"Oh, that!"

"Well?" the boy flourished his weapon, though nothing could have induced him to fire on the unarmed man.

"I was told what to do when I got here," was the reply.

"Did you see my chums on the way here?" The captive nodded.

"Where?"

"At the wreck."

"Where is your boat?" was the next question.

"On the other side of the wreck."

"And you are after the gold?"

"Of course."

"And important papers?"

"I know nothing about that."

"What is the name of your boat?"

"The Shark."

"Appropriate name that!" laughed Jimmie. "Used to be the Diver, didn't she?"

"I don't know."

"What did you come here for?"

"To get the boat."

"And remove it?"

"Of course."

"That would have meant death to the boys who are out in the water at this time?"

"I suppose so. Say, there's something wrong with your air machine. I know something about such contrivances, and this one acts as if a hose out in the sea had been cut!"

G. Harvey Ralphson

CHAPTER X

A CHASE ON THE OCEAN FLOOR

Jimmie listened for an instant. There certainly was something the matter with the air machine.

"Get a move on!" shouted the captive, "or we'll all be food for the sharks directly."

"Remain quietly where you are, then," Jimmie said, with a significant flourish at the gun which he had no intention of using, except in a case of the direst necessity.

"Go!" shouted the other.

Jimmie did not know what to do. While he had learned a good deal about the submarine, he was by no means an expert in the handling of her. His experience with the air machines had been very slight, as the boys had made little use of them.

"It's getting close in here already!" cried the captive in alarm. "Why don't you do something?"

"What is there for me to do?" asked the boy.

"Release me and I'll fix it," suggested the other.

Before Jimmie could explain the foolishness of this proposition, he heard a pounding at the outer door of the water chamber. He bounded through the open doorway and looked out.

There was a helmeted face against the pane. The boy was motioning for the door to be opened.

"Now," mused Jimmie, "I wonder how he got up there? The lifting lines haven't moved. Why didn't he let me know he was coming up?"

"Hurry!" called the captive.

Jimmie knew, from the flounderings on the floor, that the fellow was again trying to get rid of the rope. He stepped to the door and lifted a hand in warning, then slid the bolts and guards so the water chamber door would open from the outside, then stepped back into the larger apartment and closed the door.

He heard a rush of water and knew that some one was entering. Then, satisfied that all was well, he turned to his prisoner.

The fellow was half out of the rope, and one hand was sneaking toward a heavy ax which lay not far off.

"Cut that!" cried the boy.

He stood guarding the man while the water chamber filled and emptied. Then the door opened and Ned came in, helmet in hand. First, he turned a screw and the trouble at the air machine ceased.

"What the dickens!"

Ned stopped short in the middle of the room as he turned and gazed in amazement at the prisoner.

"I've been fishin'," Jimmie explained, with a chuckle.

"What is it you caught?" asked Ned.

"This," said Jimmie, "is the original sea serpent!"

"Looks to me like Moore, Jr.," Ned said.

"No?" exclaimed the boy.

"Are you the son of Captain Moore?" asked Ned.

The other nodded.

"I thought you'd recognize me," he grunted. "I was a fool to come here."

"That's about the only true word you've said since you came on board, I take it," Ned went on.

Young Moore scowled and bent his eyes to the floor.

Ned now turned to Jimmie and asked:

"Why didn't you draw us up?"

"Why," replied the little fellow, "I never got the signal."

"Guess you were too busy getting your sea serpent," smiled Ned.

"Did you pull?" asked Jimmie.

"Sure. Jack and Frank are out there now, ready to beat you up for keeping them out so long."

The prisoner turned his face away from the two and sulked.

"There's the boys now," Jimmie said. "Let them in."

In ten minutes Jack and Frank were in the large room, busily engaged in taking off their deep-sea clothes.

As Frank threw his helmet into a corner he held up the end of a line.

"You see," he said, glancing angrily at the prisoner, who had moved as far away as possible. "The line was cut."

"Aw, it would have come away in your hand when you pulled, then," said Jimmie. "You'd have found that out quick enough."

"I tell you it was cut," Frank insisted. "It was cut and tied to a rock that lies at the bottom. When we pulled we pulled at the big old boulder we saw lying there on the sand. Now, what do you think of that?"

"Why did you do it?" asked Ned, turning to Moore.

"I didn't," was the reply.

"Who did?"

"I don't know."

"I don't believe you."

"There were others besides me," insisted Moore.

Ned made an examination of the end of the three cords. All had been cut. All had been tied to something, for the ends were frayed as if by being twisted about in the hands.

"I presume you thought you were cutting the air-hose?" asked Ned, tentatively.

"I reckon I know a line from a hose," was the reply.

"So you did cut them?"

Frank sprang toward the prisoner with flashing eyes. "I'll show you what such sneaks get here."

Ned drew the enraged boy away.

"He'll get what's coming to him at some other time," he said. "Let him alone for the present."

"But he did attempt to cut the hose!" Jack exclaimed. "We ought to throw him out to the sharks."

"Not now," said Ned, coolly.

"Anyway," Frank said, a smile showing on his face, "he made us swim to the boat."

"He did that himself," laughed Jimmie, "and lost his weights."

"That's the worst of it," Jack remarked, "we've lost our weights, and there's no knowing how we are to get more."

Jimmie now pointed to the air machine.

"Was there something wrong with it?" he asked.

Ned shook his head.

"Working perfectly," he said. "There wasn't a screw loose."

"Well, he," pointing to the prisoner, "said there was something wrong, and I began to think he was right."

"Imagination!" laughed Jack.

Ned now faced Moore and asked:

"Have you taken the gold out of the wreck?"

A shake of the head was the answer.

"Have you discovered any important papers? You know what I mean by 'important.'"

"We have not."

"You came in the Diver?"

"Yes."

"Run her across?"

"No; came on a tow-line."

"I thought so. What steamer towed you over?"

"I can't answer that."

"Why?"

"I'm not permitted to."

"It was a Japanese boat?"

"Well, yes, it was."

"And she kept you out of sight all the way over and dropped you here to do this dirty work?"

"She didn't put a brass band on board of us," replied the captive, sullenly. "What is the meaning of this third degree business? Who do you think you are?"

"Your people know that we are here, of course?"

"Oh, yes, we're not fools. We saw you from the first."

"And they know where you started for?"

"Sure."

"Is your father in the Diver?"

"I refuse to answer any more questions," Moore stormed. "You've got the upper hand now, but the time will come when things will be reversed. Release me!"

"Of course," replied Ned, "we'll release you and give you the run of the boat! You came here to murder us, and so are entitled to the most courteous treatment!"

"Well, quit asking impertinent questions, then," snarled the other. "You can at least do that."

Ned hunted up two pairs of handcuffs, ironed the prisoner, and then conveyed him to a little room used for storage purposes. Moore did not appear to like this program.

"If anything should happen," he declared, "I'd be left here to die like a dog."

"And serve you good an' right!" Jimmie consoled.

"What do you expect is going to happen?" asked Jack.

"Oh, I don't know," was the hesitating reply. "Something might, you know."

The boys went out and shut the door, leaving young Moore protesting against the treatment he was receiving.

"Now," Ned said, when the boys were assembled in the large room, "it is plain that the rascals on board the Diver are preparing to attack us, or do something to imperil our lives. You saw how frightened Moore was when he was locked in that room."

"Yes, he seems to fear that he will be brought to death by his own friends," Frank said.

"What do you suggest?" asked Ned.

"Stay an' fight!" urged Jimmie.

"Hide away from them!" Frank proposed.

"Wait here until we see what they propose doing," Jack ventured.

"I think," laughed Ned, "that we'll bunch your advice and utilize it all. We'll hide in some deep spot until we see what they're up to, and then we'll fight."

"I reckon they are about five to one."

This from Frank, who preferred meeting the enemy on dry land.

"Oh, we can't come to a hand-to-hand battle," Ned replied. "We've got to fight submarine fashion."

Without attempting any explanation of this observation Ned proceeded to make a careful inspection of the boat. There was a torpedo tube at the prow, and this he studied over for a long time.

"Goin' to blow 'em up?" asked Jimmie.

"I was thinking," was the reply, "that we might use this as a bluff if we come to a tight place."

"Aw, what's the use?" demanded Jimmie. "You don't make bluffs! You get the winning hand before you call! If I had my way, I'd blow 'em out of the water!"

"Yes, you would!" Frank said. "You'd be the first one to kick if we should attempt to put that thief in there out of the boat. You're the tender-hearted little child of the bunch!"

All the boys laughed, including Jimmie, for they knew that what Frank said was the truth. Jimmie liked to talk of merciless measures, but he was not inclined to put them into practice.

"Well," Ned said, presently, "the Diver people will soon understand that something has happened to Moore, and will be after us. We may as well take a moonlight stroll."

The water tanks were filled, the power turned on, and the Sea

Lion, with no lights in sight, save the one at the prow from which Frank watched the level ahead, began feeling her way to the south.

"The charts show a deep pit not far off," Ned said, "and we'll hide there for a time and see if they give up the job of looting the wreck. The loss of young Moore may scare them out."

"Why not go to the surface and air out the boat?" asked Jack. "Our air apparatus is all right, of course, but I like the real thing better. We can drop down again in a few minutes."

"That's a good idea," Ned replied, and in a moment the Sea Lion was lifting to the surface.

In half an hour she was down again, dark and silent, in the pit of which Ned had spoken. Occasionally the submarine was lifted a few fathoms in order that anything unusual in the vicinity of the wreck might be observed.

Sometime near morning the Diver was seen making her way to the north as if setting out for a long voyage. The lights of the craft showed plainly—that is, as plainly as lights ever show at that depth—and the Sea Lion had no difficulty in following her.

"She's steamin' up!" Jimmie cried, presently. "I believe she knows we're after her."

But the Sea Lion was equal to the task set for her, and all the remainder of the night the chase went on.

G. Harvey Ralphson

CHAPTER XI

JIMMIE GOES OUT HUNTING

"I hope she'll make for some port where there is an American man-of- war," Ned said, as the sea grew shallower.

"You bet she won't," Jack replied. "She'll make for some out-of-the- way place where she can get rid of her plunder."

"Why don't we go back an' see if she took all the plunder out of the wreck?" asked Jimmie.

"If we lose sight of her now," Ned answered, "we may have hard work picking her up again. If there is anything left in the wreck it will keep. The thing to do now is to catch her and recover what she took away, then have her held to await the action of the Washington authorities."

"But we ain't catchin' her!" urged the little fellow.

"Well, we are not losing her," Jack replied, "and that is the principal thing."

"She may give us a long chase," Ned went on, "for she undoubtedly knows that we are in pursuit, so we must get ready to travel over a good deal of ocean floor before we get our hands on the thieves."

The chase went on all day and all the ensuing night. At dawn of the second day the Diver ran up into what seemed to be a little bay protected by two long points of land. The Sea Lion halted outside and waited. Once she came to the surface in order to purify the boat, and Ned took observations.

"Where are we?" Jimmie asked.

"We're here!" laughed Jack.

"This is all new land to me," Ned replied.

Frank clattered down the staircase into the bowels of the submarine and brought out a map, which he spread out on the floor of the conning tower. It was pretty crowded there, with the three boys grouped about it, for the hatch was still open.

"We've been going north all the time?" he asked.

"Just a trifle east of north," Ned answered.

"And we've been running at the rate of about twenty miles an hour for 24 hours," continued Frank. "Figure that out."

"Not far from 480 miles," cried Jimmie.

"Then measure," Frank continued. "This map shows about 400 miles to the inch. Now, where would a run of 480 miles bring us?"

"To the coast of Kwang Tung," suggested the little fellow.

"But this is an island," Ned explained, looking through his

glass. "I can see water where the main land ought to be."

"Figure it out, then," persisted Frank. "We've come to an island in the China Sea by running 480 miles a little east of north. Where would that bring us?"

"Hailing island," suggested Jimmie.

"Wise little chap!" laughed Frank. "You've hit it!"

Ned was silent for a moment. He was wondering why the Diver, or the Shark as she was now appropriately called, had put in there. Could it be that she was expecting to be met there by some vessel commissioned to remove the plunder she had taken from the wreck?

Or was it true that the plot had included a hiding of the plunder on the shore and the delivery of the documents—if any had been found—to some official of the accusing power?

These thoughts were disquieting. The boy had already missed the opportunity of searching the wreck in advance of all others, though the fault was not his own. The best he could do now was to secure the plunder from the pirates who had removed it.

In case assistance came to the people of the rival boat at that distant point, he would not be able to do this. The conspirators might hide the gold in the country near the port and deliver the papers and he would be powerless to prevent.

"I wonder," he mused, "if anything can be gotten out of young Moore? It is possible that he has been in solitary con-finement long enough to comb down that sneering attitude."

Leaving the boys on the conning tower, therefore, he hastened to the room where Moore was incarcerated, although the irons had been removed from his hands and feet.

"Well," snarled the young man, "you've come to the jumping off place, have you?"

"What do you mean by that?"

"You've chased the Shark to her lair, eh?" Moore added, with a leer.

"How do you know that we've been chasing the Shark?" demanded Ned.

"Oh, you wouldn't be running full speed unless you were after her."

"How do you know that we're not in Hong-kong harbor, ready to communicate with Washington and an American man-of-war?"

Ned thought the fellow's face turned a shade whiter as the suggestive words were spoken. However, he said nothing.

"Do you know where we are, if, as you seem to think, we have followed the Shark?" asked Ned.

"How should I know?"

Moore had evidently reached the conclusion that he had said too much at the opening of the conversation.

"You know where the Shark was headed for?" asked Ned.

"She's headed for a place where you can't butt in on her,"

G. Harvey Ralphson

answered the young man with a snarl. "When are you going to turn me loose? Aw, what's the matter with you?" he continued, assuming an air of good- fellowship. "I never did anything to you. Why can't you let me go, and say nothing about it?'

"Because," Ned answered, "you are a dangerous person to be at large. The next time you attempt to murder the crew of a submarine you may have better luck."

"Well, you keep right on," Moore scowled, "and you'll come to a place where there'll be no such word as luck in your dictionary. You might save yourself now by letting me go."

"You're a snake," cried Ned. "I wouldn't trust you with the life of a rat I cared for. Such people as you ought to be smothered at birth."

"Pile it on, now that you have the inning," said Moore. "Pretty soon you'll be playing second fiddle."

Ned went out of the temporary prison and locked the door without further talk. He had gained the point he sought.

Nothing could be clearer, now, than that the Shark was to meet fellow conspirators there. The boy was up against a tough proposition.

He believed that the Shark had secured the important papers. She would hardly have left the wreck without them.

The gold did not matter so much, yet he did not like the idea of his rival taking it out from under his very nose. He did not believe that all the gold had been secured, and figured that the Shark would go back after the remainder—but not until the important papers had been delivered to the conspirators.

In order to clear her skirts of the false accusations being whispered through foreign court circles, the Government must get possession of those documents. Ned had no idea where they were, where they had been stored, but he believed that, somewhere in the shipment of gold, full instructions for its use had been given.

The papers might have been tucked away in a keg or package of gold coins. At least they would have been placed where the revolutionary leaders could find them, and where the Chinese federal officers could not—or would not be apt to— find them in case the plans of the conspirators failed in any way.

It struck Ned as a crude arrangement from start to finish. The idea of shipping gold to the Chinese government in such a way that the revolutionary leaders were sure to seize it looked too childish for diplomats to entertain. The fact that it had miscarried was proof that it was not well conceived.

A certain foreign nation, put wise to the conspiracy, had sent a ship out to ram the gold bearing craft, and there she lay at the bottom of the China Sea, with all sorts of rumors concerning her cargo and mission circulating through Europe —greatly to the loss of Uncle Sam's reputation as a square-dealing old chap.

Ned had no doubt that the foreign government which was kicking up the most noise over the affair had sent the Shark to the China Sea to search for the papers in the hope that they would bear out the accusations that had been made. In case they did not the papers would doubtless be destroyed—and the charges would continue to be made—the charges that the subtreasury in New York had shipped the gold to aid the revolutionary junta in making a republic of China.

So it will be seen that Ned was in no position to give further attention to the wreck, or the gold it might or might not contain until he had done everything in his power to secure the papers, if any had been found, before they could be destroyed or delivered.

And now the question was this:

"How can I get to the Shark and have a look through the plunder taken from the wreck?"

The decision was that he could not accomplish such a mission. It would be impossible for him to board the Shark, or make a search even if he should succeed in getting into the rival submarine.

What next? The men on board the Shark would undoubtedly go ashore if the boat remained long in the bay. Why not land and watch about the island for the arrival of the foreign conspirators?

The island was not a large one, and there were few inhabitants, so a meeting such as Ned believed was set for the place could not fail to attract some attention. Well, the first thing to do, he reasoned, was to discover if the Shark was sending her men on shore.

"Jimmie," he said, as he returned to the conning tower, "how would you like to go hunting in the bottom of the sea?"

"Fine!" shouted the lad.

"Bring in a catfish with a bunch of kittens," Frank laughed. "I'm afraid we have mice in the provision room."

"I'll find a dogfish with a couple of puppies," replied Jimmie, "so we can have plenty of bark to build fires with."

"A bad joke," Frank replied. "If you'd quit studying up slang and read the best authors you wouldn't inflict such pain-giving jolts."

"Who's going with the kid?" asked Jack, sticking his nose up through the open hatchway.

"I am," replied Frank, calmly. "It is not safe to trust him on the island alone."

"What do you want me to hunt?" asked Jimmie, turning his back on the two boys.

"Information."

"I can get that in a book," said Jimmie, with a wink at Frank.

"Get into your promenade suit," Ned continued, "and I'll let you out on the bottom. Then I'll warp the Sea Lion around that point of land, so you can see where the Shark lies and what is going on, if anything."

"Carry me around the point of land before you drop me," suggested the little fellow.

"No," Ned answered. "I want you to search the ocean floor on the way around the point. The rascals may have laid mines there, or the people on board may be making trips to the point, just to see what we are up to. Understand?"

"Oh, yes, I see the point, all right," was the reply. "And you want me to go out in the wet and inspect another point?"

"Cut it out!" cried Jack.

Jimmie ran off, laughing, to put on his deep-sea suit, and in a moment was back asking Ned to set his helmet in place.

"When you get down to the bottom," Ned said, before attaching the heavy headpiece, "keep hold of your lifting line and signal stop or forward, just as you find it easy or difficult to make your way along the level. One jerk for stop and two to go ahead. You won't forget that. Think of the signals on the surface cars in little Old New York."

"And keep your eyes out for signs of air-hose and lines on the bottom," Frank put in.

"All right," the boy cried, cheerfully.

"You have a long air-hose and a very long line," Ned went on, "so you can go up the bay where the Shark lies quite a distance after we stop the Sea Lion at the point."

The helmet was now put on, the lad passed through the water chamber, and directly there came a signal on the line—two quick jerks.

The submarine moved slowly ahead, and Jimmie almost crawled on the bed of the ocean. The water was not very deep, not more than ten fathoms, and the bright sunlight enabled the boy to see quite well.

Fishes, large and small, sea reptiles, hideous in aspect and attractive as to coloring, swam around him, and terrifying forms rose from the bottom and rubbed against his helmet windows. He felt safer on the bottom, for then the creatures could come at him in only one way.

Presently the sand in front of him showed commotion. It stirred and clouded the water. Jimmie stopped and looked, drawing his weapon—the razor-pointed steel bar—to the front as he did so. Then he felt something close about an ankle and draw him down. A serpent's head showed on a level with his shoulder.

G. Harvey Ralphson

CHAPTER XII

JACK MAKES A DISCOVERY

"Now," Ned said, when the Sea Lion stopped in response to a quick pull from below, "who is going to shore with me?"

"Me for the shore!"

Both boys spoke at once.

"But one must remain on board," declared Ned.

"Then let Frank stay," laughed Jack. "Somehow, I always get into trouble when I am left on guard."

Frank looked disappointed, but said nothing, and Ned and Jack prepared to go ashore. When they were ready the submarine was carefully raised so that the conning tower was out of water.

The boys did not know, while they were doing this, that the signal to stop was an involuntary one on the part of the boy who was exploring the ocean floor. They did know, however, that Jimmie had a very long air-and-signal-system, and that under ordinary circumstances it could do no harm to lift the Sea Lion to the surface. The exact effect of this action on the little fellow will be seen in a short time.

When the conning tower was out of water, the point showed still ahead of the submarine, and Ned wondered why Jimmie had ordered a halt there. In one way this was an advantage, as the people at the head of the bay, if any were there, would not be able to see what was going on at the spot where the Sea Lion lay.

As soon as the hatch was opened Ned and Jack brought up a small boat and launched it. It was a narrow boat and seemed almost too small to carry two husky boys, but she was capable of harder service than that.

"Keep a sharp watch for the line," Ned warned, as they left Frank looking sadly over the rim of the tower. "Jimmie would be in a bad box down there if you should forget him."

"All right!" Frank answered, cheerfully. "I'll take care of the little scamp, but I don't believe there is water enough in the ocean to drown him!"

The boys, paddling the boat softly, proceeded to the west of the point of land near which the Sea lion had stationed herself. Ahead of them they saw a sloping shore, running white and smooth as to surface for some distance from the water. Then, at the back, rose a line of wooded hills. There were no natives in sight.

"I'd like to know what kind of people live on this island," Jack said as they landed and drew the boat up on the beach. "Whoever they are, they don't appear to have houses."

They crossed the white rim of beach, keeping their eyes on the boat as they advanced, and came to an elevation in the wild country beyond. From this elevation a small clearing showed to the east, and in the clearing were a number of buildings, some residences of a poor type and some evidently erected for business purposes.

"There," Ned said, pointing, "if we could get down into the cluster of buildings, with an interpreter, we might find out whether the Shark fellows have landed yet, and whether there are strangers loitering about the island."

"Yes," Jack answered, "the place is so small that any strange faces would be instantly noted. Suppose I skip down there and see what I can learn?"

"I think that a good idea," replied Ned, "only you're such a reckless chap that you're likely to get into trouble."

"I'll be the good little lad," laughed Jack. "You remain here and see that no one steals the boat while I size up that burg."

Jack was off, creeping through the undergrowth, before Ned could utter a warning, and the latter sat down to wait for his return. The cluster of buildings was not very far away, and Jack could not be gone very long.

Ned was pretty well satisfied with the arrangements made to corner the men who had plundered the wreck. With Jimmie watching operations from the bottom and Jack investigating from the land, it seemed to him that the robbers could not well make any important move without being observed.

In the meantime Jack was making his way toward the little town, if such it may be called, at the head of the bay. He could see people moving about in the one lane-like street, but there was no one nearer him than that—as he at first believed.

Presently, however, he heard a low whistle, coming, apparently, from a thicket just ahead. It seemed to be an amazed whistle, at that, and Jack paused in wonder.

Who could it be? If any of the people on the Shark had come onto the island they certainly wouldn't be whistling to attract his attention.

More likely, he thought, they would be lying in wait for him with a gun. What he hoped was that some American, familiar with the island and friendly with the natives, had strayed into the thicket.

Jack whistled in reply and then stepped back out of sight. He had an idea that he wanted to see the other fellow first.

Before long a voice came out of the thicket, a voice which might have come from a tenement on Thompkins Square, in the city of New York.

"Vot iss?" were the words Jack heard.

"Show yourself!" commanded Jack.

"Py schimminy," came the answer, "you gif me in the pack one, two, dree pain. What?"

"You're Dutch!" said Jack.

"Chermany!" corrected the other. "Come a liddle oudt."

Jack stepped out of the shelter and soon saw a boy of about seventeen do likewise. The boy was short, round, fat, muscular, and big and red of face. He was dressed in a checkered suit of ready-mades which did not fit him, and his blond head was covered with a cap such as German comedians use on the stage.

"Hello, Dutch!" Jack called out.

"Irish!" exclaimed the other.

Jack threw out his right hand in full salute, wondering if the German boy was a member of the Boy Scout army, and was pleased to see him make an awkward attempt to respond.

"I got it my headt in," the German said, "but I can't get it oudt. It shticks. Vot is? I'm the Owl Padrol, Philadelphia."

"No one from Philadelphia ever does remember," laughed Jack. "What are you doing here?"

The boy took himself by the back of the trousers with his right hand and by the back of his neck with the other, then bounced himself forward, as if being thrown out of a vessel or a building.

"You mean that you got fired off a ship here?" asked Jack, almost choking with laughter.

"You bet me I didt!" exclaimed the other. "I hidt in a lifeboad to get me pack to Gott's goundry, an' they foundt me. Shoo! Kick! Den I schwim! Gott un himmel! Vot a goundry!"

"Where did you get aboard the ship?" asked Jack.

"Hongkong."

"What's your name?"

"Hans Christensohnstopf—"

"Never mind the rest of it," laughed Jack. "I'll call you Hans. How long have you been here?"

Hans ran his hands around his waist as if counting time by the number of meals he had missed.

"Month," he finally said.

"Where are you stopping?"

Hans explained that there was one English trader in the place, and that he was giving him about half what he needed to eat and a place to sleep in return for about ten hours work each day.

"Do you want to get away?" asked Jack.

"Aindt it?" cried Hans. "I think I'm foolish to stay here. You schwim here?"

Jack knew that it would take a long time to make Hans understand the means of transportation he had used in reaching that part of the world, so he merely shook his head and went on:

"If you'll do something for me, Hans, I'll take you off the island."

"Me—sure!" was the quick reply.

Jack then explained that he wished to know if there were any strangers in the town, and if anything had been seen of the submarine people. Hans listened attentively.

"I'll remain here until you come back," Jack said, after concluding his instructions. "Get the information and I'll take you off the island and land you in Philadelphia."

"Sure!" cried Hans, and disappeared from view in the thicket.

Jack lay a long time watching the sky and listening to the singing leaves about him. He wished that he had instructed Hans to return to the place where he had left Ned and gone there himself to await the information he sought. The time passed heavily on his hands.

Once he moved out to the place where he had entered the thicket and looked down toward the spot where Ned was. There was a certain amount of companionship in that. He did not dare leave the thicket entirely, for fear Hans would miss him on his return from the village.

When he returned to his waiting place, after this visit, and looked down on the village, shimmering in the hot sun, he saw that something unusual was going on there. Natives, clad in the long skirts worn by many Chinamen, were flying up and down the street, and Jack recognized three Europeans mixing into the excitement.

Then he saw people running toward the little wharf at the head of the bay. Hans did not appear to be within the range of Jack's vision.

"There are doings of some kind down there," Jack mused, "and it seems to me that the foreigners created the row, whatever it is. I wonder if Hans will get out of it alive?"

The next moment Hans was there to answer for himself.

Jack saw the German lad chasing through the undergrowth as if the very Old Nick was after him, swinging his cap as he ran, and shouting out some words which he could not understand.

Finally Hans turned square about, pointed in the direction from which he had come, and resumed his flight toward Jack.

"I guess some one is chasing the boy," Jack concluded, stationing himself close to a slender path which Hans was certain to follow.

In a moment the wisdom of this remark and this arrangement became apparent. Hans came nearer, puffing and grunting, and a second after a runner who was gaining on the German shot around an angle of undergrowth and reached out for Hans.

Hans had passed the spot where Jack crouched by this time, and the pursuer was proceeding to foot it after him when Jack stuck out a leg and brought him to the ground. Hans saw the action and fell flat on the ground, blowing like a fat man on a thousand-step climb.

The man who had fallen, apparently an Englishman, middle aged, well dressed for that country, and with a red, passionate face, sat up and scowled at Jack.

"Wot the bloomin' mischief did ye do thot f'r?" he asked.

"To stop you," replied Jack.

"You're bloody roight ye stopped me!" cried the other, trying to get on his feet. "An' now I'll be stoppin' of ye!"

Jack placed his hand on the man's shoulder and pushed him back to the ground.

G. Harvey Ralphson

"Rest yourself," he said.

"You just wait, you bounder!" threatened the Englishman.

"What's it all about?" asked Jack, as Hans arose and cautiously approached.

"Don't let that bloody robber get away!" shouted the Englishman, trying once more to get up.

Jack presented his automatic, which he would not have used under any circumstances, unless his life was actually in danger.

"Keep quiet," he said.

"I'll have your head for this!" bawled the other.

"What is it, Hans?" asked Jack, paying no attention to the threat of the angry Englishman.

"I'll tell you what it is!" cried the Englishman. "That Dutch bounder stole from my safe. I chased him up here an' you took occasion to hinterfere, worse luck. Who are you, anyhow?"

"Did you steal anything from him, Hans?" asked Jack.

Hans shook his head.

Then explanations settled the trouble. A man from the submarine had met another at the trader's store. Hans, in his anxiety to hear what was being said, had crawled in behind a counter, near the safe, and had been discovered there.

The event had created no little excitement in the town, for

the chase through the street had been witnessed by and participated in by about half the population. To satisfy the Englishman, Hans was searched, and nothing found. Then Ned asked him a question:

"Where did the submarine people go?"

"Back to their boat," was the prompt reply.

"And the man who met them there?"

"He went with them."

"Where did the latter come from?"

"From Hongkong, he said."

"How long ago?"

"Something over a week."

"He was waiting for the submarine?"

"I think so."

"What, if anything, did the submarine land?"

"Nothing at all."

"You are certain of that?"

"Oh, yes, of course. The submarine man brought some sealed papers with him, and the discussion was all about them. The submarine man wanted money, I guess, and the other wouldn't give it."

G. Harvey Ralphson

"So the submarine people still have the papers?"

"Yes."

"But the other man went on board?"

"Yes, that is the way of it."

"Do you know who that Hongkong man is?"

"He is an Englishman."

"Now," said Jack, "I wish you would come down to the beach with me. I have a friend there I want you to talk with."

The Englishman, seeing that something interesting was in the air, went without objection, but when they reached the beach they saw Ned making for the Sea Lion in the boat. And just before he reached her, they saw the conning tower disappear beneath the surface of the water.

CHAPTER XIII

JIMMIE DEMANDS A MEDAL

Jimmie's first thought, as he saw the flattened head of the sea monster sliding upward toward his helmet, was that he had encountered the original sea serpent. There seemed to be a coil about the boy's leg, and he dropped down lower to see what the chances were for cutting it away with his weapon.

The prospects did not seem favorable, for his steel bar, while very sharp at the point, was not intended for chopping work. He could pierce the body of the reptile, but could not weaken its strength so that the coil would drop away.

It was when he dropped down that the spasmodic jerks on the line were given. The sea monster had included the line in his coil, and it drew as the boy bent lower.

The air-hose seemed to be clear, but Jimmie was afraid that the flounderings of the serpent might break it. The horror was certain to do some thrashing about when he felt the keen edge of the steel.

The only way was to strike some vital spot. That would end the combat at once. The serpent's head lowered with the boy, as if he had great curiosity to find out exactly what sort of a

G. Harvey Ralphson

being it was that had invaded his kingdom.

The boy was cheered by the thought that the submarine had stopped, although he did not realize at the time that the signal had been given by the action of his enemy. If the boat had continued on her course, the air-hose and the lifting line must both have been broken in a short time, as the boy's progress was stopped by the great weight of his terrifying foe. Then the end would have come instantly.

The coil about the leg was drawing tighter now, and the boy was in considerable pain. Also the coils were ascending as the head of the sea monster swung around.

It was not only the pain and the deadly danger that brought a momentary shiver to the boy. It was the fact that the repulsive body of the serpent was winding closer and closer about him.

He seemed to feel the slimy skin of the deep sea terror slipping through his waterproof suit, although his common sense told him that such could not be the case. He even thought he scented the sickening odor which he had now and then experienced in the Central Park Zoo. He knew, too, that this was purely imaginary, but the horror of a nightmare was on him, and for only an instant he lost his nerve.

Once more the head swung around and the boy presented his weapon and struck with all his might. The needle-like point entered the throat of the serpent and passed through just at the back of the long, spotted head.

There was a great switching in the water for an instant, and then the coils loosened. The blow, as Jimmie afterwards discovered, had broken the spinal cord.

While not yet dead, the serpent was incapable of moving the lower part of his body. With a sense of loathing he pulled at the coils until he was clear of them.

The water where he stood was now taking on a faint reddish hue, and Jimmie hastened away. At first, weakened and shaken as he was by the disgusting encounter, he determined to return to the submarine, then the thought of what his chums would say to him if he gave up caused him to proceed in the direction of the Shark.

He moved over the level bottom, looking for lines which would indicate that the Shark people were out watching the movements of their rival, but found none. When he came to the end of his line he signaled for the submarine to go ahead.

In this manner, by slow degrees, and always keeping his eyes out for creatures similar to the one he had vanquished, he advanced until he saw the bulk of the Shark only a short distance away. Then he called for a stop.

He remained there some moments, watching the Shark lift to the surface. Then a dark object passed shoreward, and the boy was certain that a boat had been sent to the little wharf.

"I guess that will be about all," he thought. "I've secured the information Ned wants, and may as well go back."

To tell the truth, he was delighted at the thought of getting out of the water again. His encounter with the serpent had considerably lessened his enthusiasm for deep-sea work.

The Sea Lion dropped down when Jimmie gave the signal, and he was soon in the water chamber, where he found Frank in sea dress. The two were out of the water in a short time, with the chamber empty again.

"What did you do that for?" asked Jimmie, as soon as the helmets were removed.

"Do what?" asked Frank, with a smile.

"Drop down and wait for me in the water chamber."

"Did you notice the color of the water?" asked Frank.

"Yes, down there, but up here—say," he added, "the blood of that champion sea serpent never got to the surface, did it?"

"Just enough of it to cause me to think a shark was making a meal down there," replied Frank.

Jimmie told the story of the encounter, laughing at the peril which was past, but Frank looked grave.

"We'll have to be more careful how we wander about on the bottom of the sea," he said. "It was just luck that brought you out alive. You might wound a serpent a hundred times with that steel bar and never again strike a vital spot."

"Then," Jimmie laughed, "when we get back to New York you put in a claim for a Carnegie medal for me! It would look fine on the front of me hat." "I'll have Ned make you a medal out of a fish's fin," laughed Frank.

"All right!" cried Jimmie. "It will be all right, just so it is a medal."

Then Jimmie told of what he had seen in the vicinity of the Shark, and Frank complimented him on his courage and good judgment in keeping down until he had secured the desired information.

"We know now,' he said, "that the Shark people are communicating with the shore. Perhaps Ned and Jack will learn just what they are doing there. If they do, we shall know just what course to pursue."

"What's the answer?" asked the little fellow.

"Why, if the Shark people dispose of the documents—if there were any documents in the plunder—we'll have to chase after the men who take them. The gold doesn't count."

"Yes," laughed Jimmie, "and I suppose we'll leave the Sea Lion and go over the mountains in an open boat! I'm goin' to stick to the little old Sea Lion."

"Well," Frank remarked, after a short wait, "we must get back to the spot where Ned left us."

"Never thought of that!" Jimmie cried. "He may be yelling his head off because he can't come on board."

The boys lost no time in getting back to the first position, and then lifted to the surface. The conning tower, as before, was out of sight of anyone on the bay, the point of land intervening.

As the time passed the boys became anxious about Ned and Jack. They might have returned while the Sea Lion was away, they thought, and gone into the interior thinking that some accident had happened to the submarine.

"Anyway," Jimmie declared, "Ned told us to move along as my line gave out, and he must know that we'd come back to pick him up."

While the lads speculated on the possible outcome of the

visit to the shore there came a sharp collision which keeled the Sea Lion over to port. Both were active in an instant.

"That's the Shark!" exclaimed Jimmie.

"It must be," Frank agreed.

Jimmie hastened to the stern and looked out of the plate glass panel there.

"What do you see?" asked Frank, nervously.

"It is the Shark, all right," was the reply, "and she is backing off. She may be going to ram us."

"Then it's us for the bottom," cried Frank.

"Why the bottom?" asked Jimmie.

Frank did not answer for a moment. He was still standing back of the little fellow and looking over his shoulder, out of the glass panel.

"Because," he said, "the Shark takes chances in bumping us at a considerable depth. She is higher than we are, and her prow sits a great deal above our vulnerable parts. If she strikes us when we are nestling on the bottom, her blow will glance off."

"If she knows it, then," Jimmie said, "she won't follow us down. What will she do?"

"Chase herself off."

"I hope so!" cried Jimmie.

"It beats the Old Scratch why Ned and Jack don't come," Frank said, presently. "I'm afraid something has happened to them."

"There is no use of their staying ashore," Jimmie said, "for I found out what Ned wanted to know. He asked me to find out if the Shark communicated with the shore, and I did it. He ought to know I wouldn't fall down on a little thing like that," the boy added, with a grin. "I'm the only original snake charmer!"

While this sharp exchange of ideas had been going on, Frank had been working the various levers which controlled the altitude of the submarine, and the gauge showed that she was close to the bottom as the last word was spoken.

Jimmie turned away from the panel and caught hold of a railing which ran along in front.

"Look out for the bumps!" he cried!

Then there came a shock which threw both boys off their feet. The staunch craft shivered for an instant, then righted, swaying just a little under the heavy pressure of the depth she was in.

Frank sprang to the delicate machinery which controlled the air supply and the lights. No harm seemed to have been done to them.

"The Shark can't do that again!" Jimmie said, with a sigh of relief. "We're on the bottom now, and her prow would slip over our back. The only mischief she would do would be to knock off our conning tower, and that would not disable us."

"Can you see her now?" asked Frank.

　　　　　　G. Harvey Ralphson

"Sure," replied the boy. "Her lights are on."

"What is she doing?"

"Rolling on the bottom. Say, 'bo, I believe she hurt herself when she tried to soak us."

The ex-newsboy moved away from the panel and Frank took his place as lookout.

"She's crippled, all right," the latter said, after a moment's inspection of their rival, "but I can't see what's the matter."

"Course you can't. The hurt's on the inside."

"Anyway, she doesn't seem to be able to move. I know she is trying to get off by the way the water changes around her stern."

"Bump her!" advised Jimmie.

"I reckon that would settle her," Frank replied, "but I'm not in the pirate business just now."

The boys watched the Shark for half an hour or more, and then saw her move slowly away.

"She's going toward Hongkong," Frank said, "and we may as well bid her good-by."

"Not!" exclaimed Jimmie. "We've got to follow her."

"And leave Ned and Jack?"

Jimmie's jaw fell. This was something he had not thought of. The boys were still on the island—might be in great peril.

"Well, jump up to the surface," the lad said, then, "and I'll go to the island and see what's up."

"Fine chance you'd stand!" laughed Frank.

"Bet I can go ashore an' find a Boy Scout!" returned Jimmie. "We've found 'em in every part of the world."

The Shark was still in view, her lights creating faint mists under the water, but the boys did not consider her a formidable opponent now, so they lifted to the top of the ocean.

Jimmie was first out on the conning tower. The sun was still shining brightly and the water lay as quiet as the surface of a pond on a still day.

When the boy turned to the white line of sand at the rim of the sea he saw Ned and Jack standing there with two others. He waved his hat and Jack swung back from where he stood.

"Guess they've found some one worth talking with," Frank remarked, stepping up on the conning tower.

"Guess they have," responded Jimmie, "but there's some one creeping up to 'em from the thicket," he added, lifting his glasses. "Look out, boys!" he shouted, waving one hand frantically. "Look out! There's some one makin' a sneak on you!"

"They don't catch what you say!" Frank exclaimed. "Look there!"

CHAPTER XIV

A BOY SCOUT WITH A "PUNCH"

When Ned saw the conning tower of the submarine drop out of sight he rowed over to the spot where she had gone down and tried to look into the depths of the sea.

The water was fairly clear, and he could see two great bulks below instead of one. He knew then what was taking place.

"The Shark is bent on murder," he mused. "Perhaps they wouldn't be so ready to sink the Sea Lion if they knew that the manager of the whole rotten business was a prisoner on her."

He could not see clearly, of course, but he waited and watched for some moments. Then the Shark crashed with the Sea Lion and fell off, apparently crippled.

"So that's the reason Frank dropped to the bottom!" thought Ned. "He knew the Shark couldn't get a good crack at the Sea Lion when she lay on the bottom. Wonder if the Shark is injured seriously?"

He watched until the Shark turned to the east, curving around the point of land which she had passed to the attack, then turned toward the shore. Jack was still there, and he must find him before nightfall.

Much to his surprise, he saw Jack, Hans and the Englishman, Hamblin by name, watching him from the beach. He waved his hat and shouted to them, wondering all the time where Jack had picked up his acquaintances. In five minutes he was on the beach.

"Is this the boy you wanted me to talk with?" asked Hamblin, as Ned drew up his boat and approached the group.

"The same," laughed Jack, "only you mustn't call him a boy! He's a big man in his own country."

Hamblin eyed Ned critically for a minute and extended his hand. Ned laughed as he took it.

"I've met you before!" he said.

"In a cheap lodging house on the Bowery," said Hamblin. "You were looking for a man who had robbed a bank an' made a run for it."

"Exactly," Ned said.

"An' the bloomin' moocher was in the next room to mine, an' you got him. I was bloody well glad to get the five p'un' note you tipped me then. Stone broke I was."

"You earned it," Ned replied.

"It put me on me legs again," Hamblin went on. "An' I took ship an' come out to this blasted country. I wish I was on the Bowery again, blast me eyes if I don't."

"What are you doing here?" asked Ned.

"Runnin' a bloomin' store an' scrappin' with the Chinks," was the reply. "It's a bally bad game, out here."

"Rotten!" echoed Hans.

Hamblin made a break for the German.

"You thief!" he shouted.

"Hold on," cried Jack, "let me tell you about it," and he proceeded to inform the Englishman of the exact situation of affairs.

"I thought he was a bloomin' moocher," said Hamblin, in a moment. "He acted like one."

"Who is he?" asked Ned of Jack, pointing toward Hans, who now sat on the sand with his knees hunched up in his hands.

"That's Hans," laughed Jack.

Hans threw out his hand in Boy Scout salute.

"Owl Padrol, Philadelphia!" he said.

"Looks like an Owl, eh?" asked Jack.

"He is an Owl!" roared the Englishman. "He works for me, an' he wants to sleep all day an' sit up all the bloomin' night. He's an Owl all but the wise look."

"You loafer!" cried Hans, well knowing that Hamblin would not be permitted to attack him again. "You starf mine pelly! You put bugs to sleep in mine ped! How should the nights get me sleep when the ped is one processions of pugs?"

Jack now called Ned aside and told him of the meeting of the conspirators at the Hamblin store, of the sealed packet, and of the seeming quarrel, as described by Hans. Ned turned to the Englishman.

"They met there by appointment," he asked, "the man from the Shark and the man who waited for him?"

"Yes, by appointment."

"It was about papers?"

"Yes, and gold."

"Where did the man who waited here come from?"

"Some point in China."

Jack gave a low whistle.

"China!" he cried. "I wouldn't have believed it."

"Did you know either of the men who met there—ever see either of them before?" asked Ned, then.

"One of them—a Captain Moore, formerly of the United States Navy," was the astonishing reply.

"Where had you seen him?" asked Ned, motioning to Jack to remain silent.

"He first came here on a man-of-war about six months ago."

"Well, the documents were taken back on board the Shark,

G. Harvey Ralphson

then?" asked Ned.

"Yes, I think so."

"You don't know what the packet contained?"

"Papers, they said."

"Then it's all right!" Jack cried. "We can now bunch our hits! The papers and the men we want are on board the Shark. All we've got to do is to catch the Shark!"

Just then the Sea Lion rose out of the ocean and they saw Frank and Jimmie waving to them.

"So they're all right," Ned said. "A moment ago the Shark was ramming them!"

"Why don't we go on board, then?" demanded Jack. "If there's going to be a fight on the bottom I want to be in on it. Bet your sweet life I do! Hurry on board!"

"Look a liddle oudt!" cried Hans at this moment. "They say with their hats unt hands somedings. Look a liddle oudt!"

Ned did "look a liddle oudt" just then, and saw Captain Moore and a dozen or more natives crowding through the thicket, the Captain carrying a revolver in a threatening manner.

"Stand quiet," the ex-naval officer said. "I don't intend to harm any of you. Especially you, Mr. Hamblin. I only want to know where my son Arthur is."

"I haven't got your son!" blustered Hamblin.

"Make me a search!" cried Hans.

"I'm not talking to you two," snarled the Captain. "I'm directing my talk to this sneak," pointing a shaking finger at Ned, whose muscles drew under the insult.

Hans flushed and started forward, but the natives closed about the ex- naval officer.

"Where is my son?" demanded Moore, flourishing his gun nervously.

"Where did you see him last?" asked Ned.

"That is neither here nor there," the Captain replied. "I want to know what you have done with him."

"You sent him on a dangerous mission—a mission of murder," Ned said, presently.

"I don't know what you are talking about."

"You sent him to wreck the Sea Lion."

"That is not true. I have not been on board the Shark."

"Well, some one sent him. Anyway, he came on board the Sea Lion and got caught. Now, what would you have done under the circumstances? You would have given him a banquet, I presume, if he had tried to murder you and got caught at it."

"I don't care what he has done," stormed the Captain. "I want to know where he is now."

"He's at the bottom of the sea!" Jack cut in.

The Captain staggered and turned a white face to the speaker. Ned was about to explain by saying that young Moore was at the bottom of the sea in the Sea Lion when Moore sprang toward him.

"You murdered him!" shouted the enraged Captain. "You murdered him, and I'll have your life."

He lifted his pistol and fired, but the bullet went whistling through the air instead of finding the mark intended for it. Hans, seeing the peril Ned was in, had stepped forward and landed a knock-out blow on the Captain's jaw.

"You loaver!" he shouted, standing over him.

The natives rushed forward as the Captain fell, uttering a jargon which no one understood save the trader. Hamblin saw the danger in the threatening looks of the fellows and sprang for the gun, which had dropped from Moore's hand.

He reached it not a second too soon, for a brawny native was already snatching at it. The fellow seized the trader's wrist as he lifted the weapon and uttered a few words in a menacing tone.

This was enough for Hans, who stood close by, rubbing the bruised knuckles of his right hand. He struck out again, throwing the whole weight of his body into the blow. The native went down and the others drew away from the group about him.

"Great clip!" shouted Jack, as the trader threatened the natives with the gun. "You seem to be the White Man's Hope!"

Hans rubbed the knuckles again and grinned, such a bland

grin that both Ned and Jack burst into laughter.

"You sure have a punch!" Jack went on. "Where did you get it?"

"Py the verein just," was the reply.

"You're all right, anyhow," Ned said.

The trader was now addressing the natives in a language—if it was a language—which the boys could not at all understand. They noted the result of the talk with joy, however, for the black-skinned group turned toward the village and soon disappeared in the thicket, taking the knocked out fellow with them.

Captain Moore now opened his eyes and staggered to his feet. His face was deadly pale and his eyes flashed like those of an enraged wolf.

"You shall pay for this!" he shouted.

"Jack did not finish his sentence when he told you that your son was at the bottom of the sea," Ned said, thinking that the deception had gone far enough. "He should have added that he was safe in the Sea Lion."

"Then I demand his release!" shouted the other.

"I can't bring him to you," Ned said, "but I'll take you where he is."

"And if I refuse to go?"

"You'll go just the same."

"A prisoner?"

"Certainly—a prisoner charged with piracy on the high seas."

"You're a meddling fool!" roared the Captain.

Ned paid no attention to the personal abuse of the angry man, but turned to Hamblin.

"I want to talk with you," he said, "but I must get this man on board the Sea Lion first. You'll wait here?"

Before the trader could reply, a shout came over the water from the submarine, and a column of smoke came out of the open hatch.

"I guess you've got all the trouble on the Sea Lion you need there," snarled Moore, "without taking me on board. Your ship's on fire!"

CHAPTER XV

A DESPERATE PRISONER

Just as the attention of Frank and Jimmie was called to the Captain and the natives advancing upon Ned and Jack from the thicket, they heard a great beating on a door or wall below. There was only one person in the submarine save themselves, and so they knew that it was the captive who was kicking up the row.

"He knows something unusual has been going on," Jimmie observed, "and wants to turn whatever takes place to his own advantage. Suppose we go below and see what he's doing."

"He's frightened half to death, I take it," Frank surmised. "The two bumps the Sea Lion got from the Shark must have given him the impression that we had collided with a rock or reef."

"Serves him right," Jimmie replied. "He ought to be willing to take a little of his own medicine occasionally. He tried to kill us when he came on board."

The pounding below continued, and the boys went down to the door of the room where young Moore was held captive. The noise came from within, sure enough.

G. Harvey Ralphson

"What do you want?" demanded Frank, calling loudly so that his voice might penetrate the thick door.

"Let me out!"

"You've got your nerve!" answered Jimmie.

"Let me out, please!" continued the prisoner.

"Why?" asked Frank.

"Open the door and you'll see," was the reply.

Jimmie sniffed at the air in the larger apartment and pulled Frank by the arm.

"Smell anything?" he asked.

"Something does seem queer," the latter replied.

In a second there was an unmistakable odor of burning cloth in the room, and the boys began hunting about for the source of it. The pounding on the door continued.

"Open up!" young Moore shouted. "Open up if you don't want to lose your ship."

"I'll bet the fire's in there," Jimmie ventured. "I'm goin' to open the door and find out."

He turned the key, which was in the lock on the outside, and in a second the door was open. A burst of smoke shot out into the larger apartment.

Through the thick veil of the smoke, in a corner of the room, the boys saw a spurt of flame. It was running along the floor, nipping at the fringe on an expensive rug.

When the door was opened young Moore dashed out, as if desiring to pass the two boys before they got the smoke out of their eyes. Frank caught him by the arm and held him fast.

By this time the large room where the boys stood was well filled with smoke, and Jimmie opened every avenue by which it might travel to the main hatch in the conning tower. In a few moments the interior of the submarine was comparatively free from smoke.

Jimmie took a pail of water from the tap and tossed it on the creeping flame in the little room. It served its purpose and the danger was over. Frank, still holding Moore by the arm, pointed to a chair. The young fellow seemed to have no notion of taking the seat, however, for he made a dash for the hatch, which was wide open.

In order to gain the staircase it was necessary for him to pass the place where Jimmie stood. As he came up to the boy he struck out with all his force and continued his flight—for a second.

When the boy saw him getting by, he dropped to the floor and seized him by the ankles, with the result that both were rolling about in the rich rug in no time.

"Go to it!" shouted Jimmie, as Moore tried to break away from him. "Catch him, Frank!" he continued, as the stronger man pulled away.

It was quite a neat little battle, but in the end numbers won, and Moore was ornamented with the irons once more.

"Why didn't you say the boat was on fire?" asked Frank.

"You might have smothered in there."

"Wish I had!" gritted Moore.

"Go back and do it over again," Jimmie suggested. "You can have all the time you want!"

"Why didn't you let us know at first?" insisted Frank.

"Well, if you must know," the captive replied, "I was afraid you would extinguish the fire by flooding the room, if I told what the trouble was. Besides, I thought I could get away if you opened the door."

"Did you set the fire?"

"I was lighting a cigarette, and—"

"That's enough," Frank said. "Any one who will smoke cigarettes deserves to be burned alive. Wish we had flooded the room after you got well scorched and left you in it."

"You may wish so before you have done with me," threatened the other. "I'll get you yet—both of you."

"Well, get back into the den," Frank commanded. "We have had about all the lip we can stand from you. You tried to murder Lieutenant Scott at Mare Island Navy Yard, you attempted our lives when you came to this boat, and now you set us on fire and attempt to run away. You've got a long account to settle, young man."

"You can bluff now," Moore retorted, "but that is all you can do. My father is on the lookout for you and that wise guy you call Ned Nestor. When you go back, without the gold, he'll get you good and plenty. You know it! Now lock me up and go away, for I'm sick of the sight of your impudent faces."

Jimmie forced the prisoner into his room and closed the door.

"You'll have to make a supper off that smoke!" he called out through the keyhole. "You're too fly a guy to take food to."

"I'll charge it up to you!" came back from the den.

"Nervy chap!" Frank said, as the two boys hastened back to the conning tower to see what had become of Ned and Jack.

"Cheekiest fellow I ever saw!" Jimmie added. "He really thinks he's goin' to give us the slip. He really believes we daren't do a thing to him. I'll show him!"

When the boys came in sight of the beach again they saw Captain Moore threatening Ned with a revolver. Then they saw the Captain tumble over on the sand, with the German standing over him.

"Gee!" Jimmie shouted. "Prize fight!"

"Looks like it."

There was silence in the conning tower for a second, then both boys shouted out their joy as they saw Ned and Jack getting the upper hand of Moore and the natives.

"Now they'll soon be on board," Frank observed, "and we'll find out what they've been up to."

"Bet they didn't find out any more than I did," Jimmie cried. "I'll bet they had a scrap too, and that's the only thing I wanted that I didn't get."

"Wonder who that Dutch-looking fellow is?" Frank mused. "I believe Ned is putting him into the boat!"

"I'll go a dollar to a doughnut that it's a Boy Scout!" laughed Jimmie. "Don't look the part, though, does he?"

"Why do you think it is a Boy Scout?"

"Because we've always found one. If we should go to the North Pole, we'd find one there—always busy an' ready to do a fellow a good turn, too. You know it!"

"And that big fellow, with the paunch and the important look seems familiar to me," mused Frank. "Don't you recognize him?"

"Sure," was the reply. "That is Captain Moore. Don't you remember the bluff he put up in the Black Bear clubroom before we left little old New York?"

"I believe you are right."

"Well, we'll soon know all about it," said the boy. "Ned is bringin' the Captain an' the Dutch guy off to us. Funny you'll see so many rare specimens when you hain't got no gun!"

Hans grinned delightedly when he set foot on the conning tower of the submarine and glanced inquisitively into the interior. His round, baby blue eyes protruded in wonder as they fell on the comfortably furnished apartment below.

"Jump down, Dutch!" Jimmie laughed. "There is where they make men out of Dutchmen. Don't be afraid."

"Iss dot so?" grunted Hans. "Vell, if mens iss madt dere, vy dondt you go pelow?"

"Good for you, Dutch!" cried Frank. "Hit him again. He's too fresh, anyway."

"Where did you get it, Ned?" asked Jimmie. "You'll have to bake it when we get back to New York."

"Better look out, lad," Ned replied, "this boy has the kick of a mule in his left. Let him alone."

During this short by-play Captain Moore stood scowling on the conning tower, crowded close against the boys, for the platform was a small one. He now faced Ned angrily.

"What is the proposition?" he demanded.

"I have brought you here to see your son," Ned replied. "If you'll step down the stairs I'll show you where he is."

"He ought to be at the bottom of the sea," Frank said, "for he tried to fire the boat."

"I have no doubt that he resents his treatment," said Moore. "I, myself, would sink your craft this moment if it lay in my power."

"No doubt of it," Ned said. "You've come to the end of your rope, though. All the mischief you can do now is to yourself."

Moore snarled out some reply intended to be exasperating, but which made no impression on the boys, and set his feet to the stairs. The boys followed him, but the ex-naval officer reached the floor first, and, with a bound, reached the mechanism which gave forward motion to the submarine, the prow of which was turned toward the beach.

Ned sprang forward, but the boat was already under motion. It was unquestionably the intention of the prisoner to wreck her on the beach, hoping to rescue his son and make his own escape in the confusion.

Moore struck savagely at Ned as he attempted to draw him away from the lever, but missed. In a second Jimmie had his arms about those of the Captain and they went down together.

Ned leaped to the lever and shut off the power. In three minutes more the Sea Lion must have been wrecked on the shelving shore. As it was she stopped within a few yards of the danger line.

"You're a pair of murderers!" said Ned, coolly, as he seized Moore by the throat and flung him into the room where his son was incarcerated.

Young Moore's face appeared at the door as his father was forced in, and angry words between the two followed as the door was closed.

"There'll be a social session in there now," laughed Ned. "Each one will blame the other for the predicament they are in!"

"Let 'em fight it out," Jimmie advised, rubbing a bruise on his arm, which had been somewhat injured in the fall.

Hans was now gazing about the boat with something more than curiosity in his eyes. He had observed how quickly the submarine had responded to a touch of the lever, and was actually wondering if he wasn't on board one of the magic ships he had read of in the nursery.

"Sit down outside this door and see that nothing more happens in the kick line," Ned directed, thinking to give the uneasy youth something to occupy his mind. "If they get the door open, give them one of those left-hand jolts."

With another glance about the German sat down contentedly. Then Ned went to the stern and looked out of the glass panel.

"Is the Shark still in sight?" asked Frank. "Look out to the east and you'll see her if she's anywhere about."

"I'm afraid she's too far away by this time," Ned replied.

"Then we'd better be moving!" Frank said. "I'll take the boat and go after Jack, then we'll be off."

"Don't lose any time," advised Ned.

Frank, accompanied by Jimmie, was off in the rowboat in short order, and before long Jack was on board.

"Hamblin, the trader, wants to talk with you, Ned," he said as he came down into the cabin.

"He'll have to wait until we catch the Shark," Ned said. "I'm afraid we have lost too much time now."

Jack's report had shown him that the sealed packet was still on the Shark, and it was his purpose to keep after the submarine until he caught up with her. Just what would take place then he did not know, but he was willing to take great risks in order to get hold of the packet.

G. Harvey Ralphson

He did not know what it contained, but he did know that it was claimed by the enemies of his government, that it held papers which, if brought out, might smash several international treaties. His own belief was that the packet would establish the fair dealing of the Washington officials, but this was only a matter of opinion.

While the Sea Lion was dropping down and getting under way he talked the matter over with Frank. That young man was inclined to be rather pessimistic over the matter.

"If the papers in the packet are of the sort you think they are," he declared, "they will destroy them before they will permit you to get hold of them."

"They might do so only for the fact that this is a money-loving world we are living in," Ned declared, with a smile. "Those papers, whatever they are, are worth a lot of cash to some one, and they will not be destroyed."

The submarine was soon moving swiftly through the water, only a few yards from the sandy bottom. The general direction was east, toward the harbor of Hongkong.

Just before the night fell Jack, who was on the lookout in front, peering through the glass panel, declared that the Shark, or some other submarine, was in sight.

"She's crippled, too," he cried. "She advances a few paces and then stops. They are having all kinds of trouble with her. Just lie still a short time, and you'll see her mounting to the surface."

The Sea Lion was brought to a halt, and the boys watched the dark bulk ahead with all their eyes. Their own boat was dark, but directly lights flared out ahead.

"There she goes to the top!" Jimmie cried.

"And there," exclaimed Frank, "is a signal from Hans which shows that there's something doing with the prisoners!"

G. Harvey Ralphson

CHAPTER XVI

A BLUFF THAT DIDN'T WORK

Leaving the prow, Ned hastened down a little passage and came out in the room where Hans sat, grinning, before a door behind which there was a great commotion. The pounding was incessant, and the voices of the prisoners came clearly through the solid panels.

"Open!" cried the voice of Captain Moore. "There's danger ahead for you. Open the door."

"Little he cares for our hides!" Jimmie commented. "If there was any danger he'd be the last one to warn us."

"Just a crack," pleaded Moore. "Just a crack, and I'll tell you what you are facing."

Ned opened the door a trifle and saw Moore's face there, looking almost frantic in the strong light.

"Well?" Ned asked.

"There's death for us all if you go ahead," the Captain declared. "Stop where you are."

"Soh!" grunted the German.

"Oh, I'm not pretending that I care for your rascally lives," Moore went on, vindictively. "I'd kill you all this moment if it lay in my power to do so. I'm thinking of my own safety."

"Well?" repeated Ned. "What is it?"

"The boat you are chasing has dynamite on board, and a tube gun. If you go nearer, she'll blow you out of the water."

"That's cheerful," Jimmie grinned. "Why didn't she do it before?"

"Probably because she thought to get away. I've been watching her through the little port and I know that she is now waiting for you to come up and receive a dynamite ball."

"It strikes me," Ned replied, "that she is halting because her running gear is out of whack. She rammed us not long ago and got the worst of it."

Captain Moore thrust his head close to the little opening between the casing and the door and almost screamed:

"Do you mean that she is crippled so that she can't get away from you?"

"I said that I thought she had injured herself in trying to destroy the Sea Lion," was the reply.

"Well, even if she can't get away," the Captain went on, with a change of expression, "she can blow you out of the water."

"We'll have to take our chances on that," Ned replied.

After some further talk, the boy entered the room where the prisoners were and closed the door, leaving Hans on guard outside. Captain Moore frowned as he seated himself by the port.

"It is bad enough to be confined here without being obliged to endure your company," he said.

"What a snake you would have made!" commented Ned. "I never saw a fellow loaded to the guards with venom as you are. Will you answer a few questions?"

"Depends on what they are," was the reply.

"If they will aid you, you will answer them, eh?"

"Of course."

"And if they will assist me, you won't?"

The Captain nodded.

"All right," laughed Ned. "Suppose the correct answers would help us both? What then?"

"Oh, what's the use of all this nagging?" demanded the son. "If you have anything to say, say it, and get out."

"And you're a pretty good imitation of this other snake," Ned said, glancing at the young fellow. "If you interfere in the talk again I'll put you in the dungeon and forget to feed you."

Captain Moore motioned to his son to remain quiet.

"This cheap Bowery boy has the upper hand now," he said.

"Wait until conditions are reversed."

"Captain," began Ned, paying no attention to the venom of the other, "will you tell me what the packet that was rescued from the wreck by the pirates under your command contained?"

"What packet?" demanded the Captain, surprise showing on his drawn features. "What packet do you refer to?"

"The mysterious packet you came to this part of the world to obtain. You know very well what I mean."

"We came, under contract, for the gold," was the reply.

"Yet your boat went away and left most of it on the bottom after the packet was discovered."

"She came to this harbor after supplies."

"And neglected to secure them!"

"Well, there was trouble with the trader."

"You met a Shark man, on the island?"

"Of course. I came here to meet him, to receive a report as to the success of the expedition."

"You received such a report?"

"Yes."

"You were told that the gold had been found intact?"

"That is not for discussion here."

G. Harvey Ralphson

"You were astonished when your son did not make his appearance?"

"Frankly, yes."

"You expected that he would bring you the report?"

"Yes; he was in charge of the Shark."

"If he had been in charge when the man landed, he would have given you the packet?"

"If he had had a packet, or anything else taken from the wreck, he would have turned it over to me."

"But the man you met refused to do so?"

"How do you know what took place?"

"That is immaterial, so long as I do know. Tell, me, what was the difficulty at the store—money?"

The Captain did not answer.

"Now," Ned went on, "you stated a moment ago that you came here under contract to get the gold. Who are your principals?"

No reply was received.

"What will the man now in charge of the Shark do with the packet he refused to deliver to you?" was the next question.

"He will transfer it to me as soon as we meet again."

"You are sure of that?"

"Reasonably sure."

"Then what will you do with it?"

"Anything given to me will be turned over to my principals."

"But, suppose the contents of the packet are not favorable to your side of the case? Suppose they clear the United States Government of suspicion?"

Captain Moore gave a quick start of amazement.

"I don't know what you are talking about," he said.

"In that case," Ned went on, "I presume you will destroy the papers? If you can't entangle the Government that fed you so long in some trouble, you won't play."

"You've been reading some of the red-covered detective stories, and think you're a sleuth!" snarled the Captain.

"You may as well tell me all about it," Ned urged.

"I have told you all I know about the condition of the wreck."

"And the packet?"

"There was a long envelope, but I did not see what it contained."

"Yet you came here to make sure that it should not get out of your hands unless it would aid you in your treachery?"

The prisoner was silent.

"Why didn't you obtain a knowledge of its contents?"

"The man who held it refused to make delivery."

"In other words, he demanded more money than you were authorized to pay him?"

"I have nothing to say about that."

"He took the packet back to the Shark?"

"Of course."

"And made an appointment to meet you at Hongkong?"

"It does not matter to you what our arrangement is."

"Oh, yes it does, for I'm telling you now that the appointment will never be kept."

"You don't know what peril you are in this minute," snarled the other. "There are bombs under your keel now!"

Ned did not like the tone of satisfaction in which the words were spoken. The Shark had passed slowly over the spot where the Sea Lion now lay, and torpedoes and bombs might have been laid.

"Thank you for the hint," he finally said. "I'll go out and see about it."

"When you want further information," frowned the Captain, with a scornful laugh, "come in and I'll give it to you—just as I have on this occasion."

"No trouble to show goods!" broke in the son.

Ned opened the door and motioned to Hans and Jack, who were just outside, watching and listening to such few words as came through the heavy panels of the door.

"Take this impertinent young murderer to the den," he said, as Hans and Jack stepped up, "and leave him there in darkness. Don't feed him until I give the word."

The young man's struggles only increased the violence which was used in his removal. The boys would have killed the man who had attempted the lives of all the crew if they had been directed to do so.

Then Ned turned back to the Captain, now foaming with rage and calling to his son to remain docile until his turn should come.

"You pride yourself on having put me off without any information whatever," the boy said. "You advise me to come again and meet with the same treatment. Now, let me tell you, for your information, that I came in here to get answers to only two questions."

"Did you get them?"

"Indeed I did," was the reply.

The Captain looked disgusted.

"What were they?" he asked.

"I wanted to know if the man who landed from the Shark had the packet, and if he took it back on board with him. You gave me the information I sought. You even told me that the packet had not been opened when you saw it."

The Captain stormed up and down the little room in a towering rage.

"If I could turn a lever now and blow us all into eternity," he shouted, "I would do it!"

"Your mind seems to run on blowing up somebody."

Moore gritted his teeth and made no reply.

Ned locked him in again and went out to Frank, who was in charge of the boat.

"Get her over to the west a few yards," he said. "Our friend the Captain says the Shark is sowing torpedoes along here, and we can't afford to be blown up just now."

"The Shark is at the surface now," Frank said. "Anybody on the bottom?"

"Not so far as I can see, but it is pretty thick down here."

"Why not go to the surface?" asked Jack.

"Yes; she knows we are here, all right," Frank added.

"Well, keep to the bottom until you change position, then come to the top and keep dark. Not a light in sight, understand, and the tower up just high enough to keep out the water."

"What are you going to do?" asked Frank.

"I want to get aboard the Shark," was the cool reply.

"Yes; I see you doing it," Frank said.

"I can only try," was the reply. "The boat is headed for Hongkong, where she is to deliver the packet we want. She is to deliver it to Captain Moore on the payment of a certain sum of money, but if the Captain is not there she will turn it over to whoever has the price. We can't allow that."

"Of course not; but how are you going to get on board the Shark? If you don't watch out you'll be served as you served young Moore."

"The minute the Shark strikes Hongkong," Ned replied, "we will have a thousand places to search for those papers. Before she lands, we have only one."

"You are always right!" cried Frank. "When are you going to make the attempt?"

"That depends. In the meantime, we must get to the surface and in a position where we cannot be seen. If she thinks we have gone away, so much the better."

"I guess our little picnic isn't over with yet!" laughed Frank. "Are you going to take me on board with you?"

"I'll be lucky if I can take myself on board," was the reply.

By this time the Sea Lion was some distance from the Shark, and the hatch in the conning tower was open. It was a clear, starlit night, and there would be a moon later on.

There seemed to be great confusion on board the Shark. The boat was brilliantly lighted, and the conning tower stood high above the water. The ports on the side toward the Sea Lion were open, as if to admit the pure, cool air of the night.

"I believe there's something the matter with her air supply,"

Ned said to Frank as the two stood together on the tower. "The ramming she gave us must have done her a lot of mischief. Looks like she was stuck there until help comes."

"The help she ought to have is right here," Frank replied. "I'd like to get that crew on board a man-of-war."

"We have the real criminals," Ned replied.

The boys watched the Shark for a long time. They could see people moving about on the inside, and occasionally a group assembled on the conning platform, which was much larger than that of the Sea Lion.

"I believe some one is going down in a water suit," Ned said, presently. "The water chamber is on the other side, but she lists as if a weight was pulling at her."

"Listen!" Frank cautioned. "There's the machinery working. That would be the lowering apparatus. Some one is going down, all right. Now, what for?"

Ten minutes passed, and then the waters surged about the Sea Lion, and a great roar and rumble came with the waves which swept into the open hatch. The Shark, too, rocked on the crest of a great wave.

"Dynamite below!" Ned said. "Will there be more than one?"

CHAPTER XVII

BAD FOR THE SEA CREATURES

As Ned spoke there came another upheaval of water, and a louder roar from the sea. The Shark and the Sea Lion both swayed perilously. Ned and Frank closed their hatch and clung to the railing around the conning tower platform.

"Those are torpedoes, all right," Frank said.

"But I don't understand—"

Ned cut the sentence short as a third reverberation came from beneath the water.

"They think we are down there yet!" Frank said. "I wonder how the man who went down came to make such a mistake?"

"Cheerful sort of people to fight!" Ned said. "Every man on that boat is a murderer at heart."

A pounding on the under side of the hatch was now heard, and Jimmie's face showed when it was lifted.

"Say," the little fellow said, "Captain Moore wants to speak to you, Ned. These here earthquake shocks have got him goin'. He acts like a crazy man."

Ned paid no attention to the request.

"He wants to say that he told me so," Ned said to Jimmie. "Go back and tell him that he ought not to be afraid of his friends on board the Shark."

"Gee!" the little fellow replied. "If he don't behave himself, I'll turn the hose on him. He ought to have a salt water bath, anyway. For a long time he's been tryin' to give us one!"

"Let him alone," Ned ordered.

This second upheaval of the water had swung the Shark around so that the door to the water chamber was in view from the Sea Lion. The boys saw that it was open, probably left in that way for the return of the man who had gone down in the water suit.

The light, shining from the main cabin, filtered through the chamber, which was, of course, under water, only a few inches of the conning tower of the submarine now being above the surface.

"Can they shut that door from the cabin?" Frank asked.

"I presume so," Ned replied. "They ought to be able to shut the door and empty the room as well."

"That can't be done on the Sea Lion," Frank said.

"No, but that is a detail that was overlooked in the construction of the boat. I was just learning to run the craft, and did not observe the deficiency."

"Well," Frank went on, "they are closing the door, but they are not doing a good job at it. Say," he added, grasping Ned's arm, "I'll bet the machinery connecting with the door from the cabin is broken!"

"Then the man who is down below will have to come up and do the opening after he gets up, and after he shuts the outer door and exhausts the water."

"I don't believe the outer door can be closed."

"What I'm interested in just now," Ned said, "is whether the diver is still alive. If he was anywhere near where the torpedoes exploded he is dead."

"And the Shark can't close her water chamber! I see a chance, Ned," Frank exclaimed. "Suppose I drop out and enter that water chamber?"

"What for?" asked Ned.

"Why, they would think I was the other fellow and let me in."

"With your line and hose unconnected with the mechanism inside?" asked Ned.

"Never thought of that."

"The only way for us to get into that boat," Ned went on, "is to get in from the top."

"But how?"

"That's just what I'm trying to study out."

"I presume the man who went down is there for good," Frank suggested.

"He probably went down to see why the torpedoes didn't go off and got caught," Ned replied.

"Perhaps the Shark will go down to see about it directly," the other ventured.

"I hardly think she could lift again with that water chamber door open and the chamber full of water," Ned went on. "It is my opinion that they will remain on top."

"I should think she'd be afraid of the traps she set for us, anyway. I wish she would get caught in one of them."

"Not while she has that mysterious packet on board," smiled Ned. "We have traveled a long way to get that."

No more submarine explosions came, and the boys sat on the dark conning tower until nearly midnight, watching the people on the Shark flying about, evidently laboring under great excitement.

The diver had not returned. The machinery was evidently out of order and the Shark might as well have tied to the bottom for all the speed she could make.

"I'm afraid some ship friendly to these pirates will come along," Ned said, after a long silence. "I think I'd better go aboard the Shark and find out what she intends doing."

"I see you doing it!"

"I can only try."

"And try only once," Frank muttered.

"I think they are ready for a compromise by this time."

"Well, then, I'll go with you," Frank decided.

"Get up the boat, then."

Jack and Jimmie were not inclined to favor the scheme, but they assisted in launching the boat and stood with half-frightened faces while Ned and Frank stepped into her.

Just as they were pushing off, Hans made his appearance on the little platform, his china-blue eyes filled with excitement.

"Mine friendts," he said, "vot iss if I goes py the poat?"

"No more room," said Frank.

"Now, you hold on," Jimmie called out. "You know what sort of a left hand punch this baby has? Well, then, you may need him when you get over to the Shark. See?"

"That might be," Frank muttered, looking inquiringly at Ned.

"Then let him come along," the latter said, so Hans entered the boat and took up the oars. "Rows like a steam engine!" Jimmie observed as the boat sped away. "That Dutchman is stronger than a mule."

It was still and lonely on the Sea Lion after the departure of the boys. The lights of the Shark were in sight, but they did not bring cheerful thoughts. The boys sat on the railing of the conning tower and waited in no little anxiety.

Occasionally the pounding of the prisoners reached their

ears, but they paid little attention to it.

"They are suffering the tortures of the lost," Jack said. "Every minute they think they're going to the bottom. Let them take their medicine!"

"I wish they were going to the bottom," Jimmie responded. "When we see snakes like they are we ought never to let them get away from us. If we don't get bitten, some one else will."

Jack rested his chin on his palms and regarded the boy quizzically for a moment.

"How do you like it, as far as you've got?" he asked, then.

Jimmie looked down into the interior of the submarine, out over the sea, sparkling in the moonlight, then up to the heavens, bright with stars. Presently he answered:

"I don't like it."

"Why not?" "We ain't havin' any fun. We've been down in that old hold for a long time, and haven't got anywhere. I'd rather take a trip through South America, or through China. I want the ground under my feet part of the time, anyway."

"It seems to me that it is getting stale and unprofitable," Jack admitted. "Suppose we get up power and drift up closer to the Shark. Then we can at least see what's going on."

"All right, 'bo!" cried Jimmie, starting down the stairs.

"Well," called Jack, "don't be in such a hurry! We want to make sure that Ned has attracted the attention of the Shark people before we move. If they see us moving up on them before Ned gets a chance to talk with them, they may do something rash to the boys."

"Guess you are right," Jimmie admitted.

"So far as I can see," Jack continued, "they are over there now. Do you hear that voice?"

"Ned's, all right."

The boys listened, but the voice came no more.

"They've pulled him into the boat!" cried Jimmie. "Hurry up and get started!"

When Jack went below to handle the motive power machinery he heard Captain Moore thumping on the door of his prison.

"What do you want?" he demanded.

"Come to the door."

Jack did as requested, but did not open the door.

"Now, what is it?" he asked.

"Is that Nestor?"

"It's Jack," was the reply.

"Well, ask Nestor if he'll let both of us go if well give up the whole scheme. Will you?"

"And the papers?"

"I'll help him get the papers."

"I'll tell him," said Jack.

"Send for him at once," urged the Captain. "If we remain here much longer, we'll be blown out of water. You heard those explosions?"

"They harmed no one but the sea creatures," Jack replied. "They were bad for them."

"Where is Nestor?" was then asked.

"Visiting on the Shark," was the reply.

"If they've got him, he'll never come back," gritted the Captain.

"But they haven't," said the boy. "We're going to run the Sea Lion over to the Shark now and help them entertain him."

"You're a fool!" roared Moore. "Don't you tell them that we are on board—my son and myself."

"Don't they know it?"

"How should they know it? Don't you tell them. If you do they will raid your ship and get us."

"So you've been playing some dirty trick on them, have you?" asked Jack. "Well, what about your meeting them at Hongkong?"

"That was a lie."

"You are out with them?"

"They are out with me. They claim I am keeping them out of a lot of money. Don't tell them I am here."

"In all your life"—asked Jack—"in all your life, did you ever do business with any man, woman, or child you didn't cheat and betray? You ought to be hanged."

"If Nestor comes back, you send him here and I'll tell him the whole story if he'll let us go. And I'll tell him how to get the papers he is after. Will you see that he comes—if he gets back?"

"I think it would do you more good," laughed Jack, "to have a talk with the people on the Shark."

Ignoring the prisoner's further demands, Jack turned on the power and directed the Sea Lion toward the Shark. In a moment Jimmie called down through the hatchway:

"Slow up, now, unless you want to bunt the other boat."

Jack, accordingly, shut off the power and went up to the platform. The boat was still drifting ahead a trifle, and the boy went below again and dropped an anchor.

If the advance of the submarine had attracted the attention of those on the Shark's conning tower they gave no evidence of the fact. The boat Ned had taken lay swinging on the easy sea close to the tower, with Frank and Hans sitting near the stern.

Directly voices came from the other submarine. The first speaker was Ned, then a heavier voice exclaimed, angrily:

"You have no right to suppose anything of the kind. We are here on legitimate business, and must not be interfered with."

"What did you take from the wreck?" asked Ned.

"What is it to you?" came the stronger voice. "You can't make any bluff work with me."

"Then I may as well go back to my ship," Ned said.

"Go back to your ship!" snapped the other. "Not if I know myself. You have come aboard without leave or license, and you'll stay until we get good and ready to let you go."

The boys saw Hans and Frank spring for the platform, and then a shout of triumph came from half a dozen throats. Ned surely was in trouble.

CHAPTER XVIII

"MAKING A GOOD JOB OF IT"

"I guess they've got Ned!" Jimmie cried, as the heavy hatch of the Shark closed with a slam. "If they have, we'll ram 'em to the bottom."

"You just wait!" Jack advised. "There's a good deal of a racket going on over there. I guess Hans is putting his educated left into motion. Look at him!"

There was indeed a great commotion on the platform. Presently the hatch was lifted and one of the contestants disappeared.

"Do you mind that, now!" shouted Jimmie. "Ned has captured the boat for keeps! There! Now he's tellin' them where to head in at!"

Through the still night air they heard Ned's voice:

"You people down there know what I am here for. If the thing I want is destroyed you'll all be hanged for piracy. Understand?"

Then the hatch was jammed down again, and Ned and Frank

stepped into the rowboat, leaving Hans on the platform. Jimmie threw up his cap when the two boys stepped on the Sea Lion's platform.

"You captured the bunch!" he yelled, "and you stole the boat. You sure made a good job of it."

"What's the proposition?" asked Jack.

"I thought I'd tow the old tub into a port where I can communicate with an American man-of-war," replied Ned.

"This is luck!" Frank exclaimed. "Luck for us, and trouble for the pirates. I wonder if they've got much gold on board."

"If they have," laughed Ned, "Hans will see that they don't get away with it. They're nailed down hard."

"Talk about the luck of the British army!" roared Jack. "It is blind adversity to the luck of the Boy Scouts! Here we've got the pirates bunched! As soon as we communicate with a man-of-war, we'll turn 'em over to Uncle Sam and go back and get the gold."

"The Shark," Frank observed, "was a derelict when we picked her up, wasn't she? She couldn't move a foot. Well, then, we're entitled to salvage. We'll put in a bill that will eat up the whole business!"

"If we get her into port," Ned replied. "The old tub is in bad shape owing to the bunting she gave the Sea Lion. I'm afraid she'll go down before morning."

"Cripes!" Jimmie broke out. "What will we do, then, with all them bold, bad men? We've got our penitentiary full now!"

"And the prisoners are making all kinds of trouble, too," Jack added. "If the door wasn't good and strong, it'd be in splinters by this time. That young Moore is the worst."

"We won't cross any bridges until we come to them," Ned remarked. "The Shark may last until we get to Hongkong. Anyway, I'm counting on quite a run before she goes down."

"How many are there on board?" asked Jack.

"Six, not counting Hans. I think we can accommodate them all on board the Sea Lion, if we have to."

The Sea Lion towed the Shark all through the night, keeping to an easterly direction with the idea of going to Hongkong, something over 150 miles away. All along the eastern coast of Kwang Tung, from the slender peninsula which separates the Gulf of Tongking from the China Sea to the bay which penetrates almost to Canton, there is a succession of little islands, so the submarine and her prize were always in sight of land.

Just at dawn there came a cry from the platform of the Shark, and Hans was discovered waving his cap excitedly in the air.

"Vater! Vater!" he cried. "Dis iss droubles! Make us off dis durdle—gwick!"

"Sinking?" Ned called back.

Further talk with the German informed Ned that water was seeping into the different compartments of the Shark, and that the inmates were already perched on tables and on the stairs leading to the platform.

The boy attached the towing cable to a windlass on the

platform of the Sea Lion, turned on the power, and the sinking craft soon lay alongside. She was indeed in a bad predicament. Another half hour would see the last of her.

"Now," Ned said, "we don't know what those fellows will try to do when the hatch is lifted. I've known snakes to sting the hand that fed and warmed them. Anyway, we'll take no chances."

Following his orders, the boys got out their automatic revolvers and ranged themselves on the platform. Then Ned lowered the rowboat, making a bridge between the two. The hulls of the boats met under water, but the platforms, owing to the bulge, were some little distance apart. The railings of the conning towers were not much above the surface.

His arrangements for securing the prisoners without trouble completed, Ned went over to the Shark and lifted the hatch. He was greeted with a chorus of threats, supplications, and questions.

"You'll get yours for sinking the Shark!" one shouted.

"For God's sake let us out; we are drowning!" whined another.

"What's the matter with the boat?" asked a third.

"Listen," Ned said. "The Shark may go down in ten minutes, or she may float, under tow, for a long time. Anyway, you are better out of her. I'll take you all out if you promise to behave yourselves. Come out of the hatch one at a time and be searched for weapons. The man that carries a weapon of any kind on his person will be thrown back, to feed the fish. Do you understand?"

They understood, and not even a penknife was found when search was made. Five of the rescued ones were plain seamen, with little knowledge of submarine work. The other was the captain of the Shark. Under the direction of young Moore he had attempted to make off with everything of value on the wreck, including the papers.

This man was a fair type of marine officer, had, in fact, resigned from the United States service with Captain Moore. He was by no means an ill-looking man, but his snaky eyes and treacherous mouth told Ned to look out for him.

He came out of the hatch last and was stepping onto the rowboat when Ned stopped him with a question:

"Where are the papers?"

"What papers?" snarled the other, Babcock by name.

"The papers you took from the wreck."

"They are below, soaked with water."

"Get them!"

"But—"

"Get them! Quick!"

"But they are afloat, and—"

"Get them!"

Babcock went down the staircase with murder in his eyes. He returned, in a moment, with a sealed packet, which was perfectly dry. Ned broke the seal and glanced at the sheets inside.

The one which met his eyes first was headed:

"General instructions, to be opened only when the demand for the coin is made."

"Now" Ned went on," where are your sailing orders?"

"Lost!" was the reply.

"Get them!" Ned said, quietly.

"They are—"

"Get them," came again from the boy's lips.

Again Babcock went into the submarine, now rapidly filling with water. He returned dripping with sea water, holding in his hand a water-tight tin box which was secured by a brass padlock.

"You now have everything I held concerning the mission of the boat and the disposition of the gold," he said. "I suppose I may get out of the water now?"

Ned stepped aside and Babcock passed over to the Sea Lion. Ned attached a buoy to the tower of the Shark and cut loose from her.

"We'll let some of Uncle Sam's boats pick her up," he said. "I'm for Hongkong with these papers."

The five sailors were not locked up, but were given the run of the cabin, the machine room only being closed against them.

"I'm not going to have them mixing things down here," Jack, who was in charge that day, said.

Babcock, however, was locked up with Captain Moore. When the door closed on the two men the boys heard them both talking at the same time, and their language was not at all complimentary to each other.

"You're a blackmailer!" Moore yelled.

"You're a liar!" was the reply.

"Fight it out!" Jimmie shouted from the door.

"Get to going and see who's to blame for this!"

Then the voices quieted down, and no more words were heard.

"Did you hear what they called each other?" asked Jack. "Well, I'm betting they are both right."

Ned went to his cabin and opened the tin box. He lingered over what he found there until noon and then called Frank into conference with him.

"There's a plot which involves officers at Canton," he said, "and we may as well bag the whole bunch."

"Of course. We ought to make a good job of it, as Jimmie says."

Ned examined his map and called Frank over to the table where it was spread out.

"If we go to Canton," he said, "we'll have to run into the

lake-like mouth of the Si River. Guess that's its name. It looks dim on the map. Fifty miles to the north the little stream on which Canton is situated runs into the larger stream.

"We can run to that point and leave the Sea Lion while we go to Canton. I guess the prisoners won't object to a few days more of imprisonment. Anyway, we may meet a ship we can turn them over to."

"They are objecting, right now, it seems," cried Frank, opening the door and looking out into the main cabin. "Hans is sitting on one of the sailors and Jack and Jimmie are holding the others back with their automatics."

Both boys leaped out. The sailors, doubtless alarmed at the arrival of the leaders, sprang for the hatchway. The boys did not fire at them as they passed, and directly splashes in the sea told those on the stairs that the sailors had leaped into the water.

Hans arose, scratching his head, and looked down on the man he had been sitting on. The fellow looked up into the lad's face with a queer expression in his eyes.

"Vot iss?" demanded Hans. "Go py the odders if you schoose! Py schimminy, dose shark haf one feast!"

"Not on your life!" cried the prisoner. "I'm not anxious to get away. I was shanghaied on the Shark, and it's glad I am to be out of that bum crowd."

Jimmie, who had followed the sailors to the platform, now came back with the information that three of them had been picked up by a native canoe which had now disappeared from sight in a group of islands. The other, he said, had gone down.

"How much do those sailors know?" asked Ned of the man Hans had taken prisoner.

"They know a lot," was the reply. "They were all in together. What one knew, all knew, I guess. It is too bad they got away, for they had a definite plan to operate if there was trouble and any got away. They will lay in wait for you when you land."

"They'll have to travel fast if they do!" Frank laughed.

CHAPTER XIX

ON THE EDGE OF DISASTER

The Si River is not a river at all where its waters flow into the China Sea. It is a wide, salt-water inlet, a bay, a great delta, like that of the Amazon. This great bay is miles in width in places and extends at least fifty miles into the interior.

Almost at the end, it is joined by a narrow little stream upon which Canton, the capital city of Kwang Tung, is situated. The city is something less than fifteen miles from the mouth of the river upon which it stands.

It was for Canton that the boys were headed. Some of the papers Ned had found in the private box of Captain Babcock made reference to a place of meeting there which the boy desired to investigate. He was now convinced that the plot against the Government had been a vicious one, backed by people of influence and standing in the world of diplomacy. It would bring the case on which he was working to a very satisfactory finish if he could include in his report the story of a meeting of the conspirators.

While the boy sat alone on the platform of the conning tower that evening the sailor who had remained on board the Sea

Lion at the time of the escape of the others came to him. The fellow was an American, and seemed to be honest in his desire to assist Ned.

"The men who escaped," he said, "will not lose track of the Sea Lion. There are men on shore who will send the news of what has taken place on faster than you can travel. Wherever you go they will be waiting for you, and they are a bad lot."

"They have plenty of money behind them, I presume?" asked Ned.

"They appear to have," was the reply.

"Especially with the prospect of the loot from the wreck in mind," Ned suggested.

"They didn't get much gold out of the wreck," explained the other. "They pulled the yellow boys out until they came to the sealed parcel, and then they made off."

"They knew that we were on the ground, watching them?"

"Oh, yes, but they had a plan for getting rid of you."

"The plan young Moore attempted to carry out?"

"Yes."

"That meant murder?"

"Yes."

Ned was silent for a moment, thinking gratefully of the resourcefulness of the ex-newsboy. To this they all doubtless owed their lives. He promised himself that the lad should be properly remembered when the time of settlement with the Government came.

"Do you know where the conspirators are to meet at Hongkong?" he then asked.

"At Canton, I said," answered the other, with a twinkle in his eyes. "You thought to trip me?" he asked.

Ned, in turn, smiled quietly. He had indeed been testing the man.

"Well," he added, "do you know where they are to meet at Canton?"

"Oh, I heard the name of the street, but it sounded more like the clatter of falling crockery than a name, so I don't remember it."

"Perhaps a landmark was mentioned?"

"Yes, come to think of it, there was. The place of meeting is in the rear of a curio shop next door to an English chop house. That ought to be easy to find."

The visit to Canton promised to be a dangerous one, especially as the men who had escaped would send on word of what had taken place on the Shark. The fellows had been picked up by natives in canoes, and were probably at that time on the main land, within reach of a telegraph wire, or some other means of communication with Canton.

While the boy studied over the matter Frank came on the platform and the seaman went below. Ned laid the proposition before the newcomer.

"Well," Frank said, "you have the papers, you have the private orders of Captain Babcock, of the Shark, and you have the two main rascals, Captain Moore and his precious son. What more do you want?"

"I want the foreigner who put up the job."

"That does seem worth while," Frank mused.

"It's this way," Ned went on. "The sealed packet doubtless contains instruction to one of the revolutionary leaders regarding the disposition of the money. You see, they were sure the rebels would be on hand to grab the shipment as soon as it left the ship. The loss was to fall on the Chinese government and the revolutionists were to profit by it.

"The instructions make it look mighty bad for our Government, for the gold was drawn directly from the subtreasury the day it was shipped. It looked as if we were plotting against a friendly government."

"I see."

"But some one leaked. The story of the shipment got out, and the vessel was rammed one night by a steamer which has never been identified. The idea, of course, was to prevent the revolutionists getting the money, without telling what was known, or bringing the nation which butted into the case into prominence at all."

"Then some nation friendly to the Emperor of China did that?"

"I don't know. Anyway, the nation that did it bribed Captain Moore and Captain Babcock to get the gold—and to recover the sealed packet. With this in their hands, they might have made Uncle Sam a great deal of trouble."

"I understand, and now you want to get the men who conspired with the Moores and Captain Babcock?"

"That's the idea, not so much in the hope of bringing them to punishment as to locate the source of their inspiration."

"Then, I reckon well have to go to Canton," Frank remarked. "We'll see the town then, anyway."

The boy remained silent for a moment and then asked:

"What can you do to the chief conspirators if you catch them?"

"Nothing. I can only file my report with the government and drop out of the case."

"And the Moores and Babcock?"

"I'll turn them over to the first American man-of-war I meet."

"And then go back after the gold?"

"That depends on instructions."

"That's the difficulty of working on diplomacy cases," said Frank. "We have to take all manner of risks, and then, sometimes, see the real rascals get off free—on account of international complications. I'd like to work on a real old detective case on the Bowery."

Ned laughed softly but made no reply.

The Sea Lion made slow time, for the crippled Shark—

which still floated—rolled and tumbled heavily—in her wake and the sea was rougher than it had been before for many days. At last, however, she entered the long inlet leading up to Canton and cast anchor.

"Ever been in these waters?" Ned asked of the American sailor.

"Sure," was the reply. "That is why they shanghaied me in San Francisco."

"How far can I go up?"

"Clear to the mouth of the river."

Proceeding leisurely, the Sea Lion passed up the inlet. It was early morning when she came to the mouth of the river. They had passed many vessels on the way, some native, some foreign, but had not been molested, though many curious eyes were turned toward the tow and the odd-shaped craft doing the pulling.

When anchor was cast in a little bay at the mouth—a quiet little stretch of water sheltered by old warehouses which had been erected years before by native traders—Jack came running up the stairs to meet Ned.

"Captain Moore," he said, "is weeping himself to death for lack of your sweet society. He's all running out under the door!"

"Jack," Ned laughed, "if your imagination wasn't too strong, you'd do well writing fiction. As it is it is so strong that anything you might put on paper would not be believable. Anyway, I'll go and see what the Captain has on his mind."

Captain Moore had fear on his mind. Ned saw that the second the door was open. His face was white as paper and his eyes roved about like those of a madman. "You are going on to Canton?" the Captain asked, in a trembling tone of voice.

"I was thinking of it," Ned answered.

"When?"

"To-night."

"And leave the submarine here?"

"If I could take her with me," smiled Ned, "I would do so, but I'm afraid I can't."

"This is no joking matter," snapped Moore.

"I knew you would begin to look at the matter in that light before you had done with it."

"You are going to the chop house in Canton?"

"I hope to be able to find it."

"Alone?"

"Of course not."

"Well," the Captain added, wiping his dry lips with the back of his hand, "do you know what will happen to the Sea Lion while you are gone?"

"Nothing serious, I hope."

"She will be blown up, and me with it!" almost screamed the Captain. "The power that is handling this matter would do more than that to get the papers you have secured out of the way, and to get rid of Babcock, my son, and myself."

"They seek to murder you?"

"I believe it."

"Why?"

"For two reasons. We know too much, and we failed."

"You haven't named the power," suggested Ned.

"I am unable to do so. I don't know. I have done all my work with a go-between."

"I see," Ned said.

"If you must go to Canton," the Captain went on, "first turn us over to the authorities here—to the American consul, if you please."

"That would protect the boat?"

"It would protect us."

"For the present, yes."

"And take the papers with you!"

"Why?" laughed Ned, thoroughly amused.

"Because that will draw the search off the boat."

"Then you believe that I shall be watched and followed?"

"Yes, and killed."

"You're a cheerful sort of fellow!" laughed Ned.

Jimmie now came to the door and announced a warship flying an American flag.

"She's signaling you," he added.

Ned was pretty glad to see the ship come to a halt lower down the inlet. She was not a large vessel, but she looked as big to Ned as all Manhattan island.

In an hour he was on board the ship, in earnest conversation with the captain, who had been ordered by cable to look the Sea Lion up and report to Ned. In another hour the prisoners were on board the warship, and the Sea Lion was anchored under her guns.

CHAPTER XX

AN ENDING AND A BEGINNING

Captain Harmon, of the warship Union, was a brave and capable officer. He understood at once the necessity for the trip to Canton. The conspirators must be identified. The United States Government must be informed as to the foreign power which had so nosed into her affairs.

"The power that is doing this," the Captain said, "will resort to other tricks when this one fails. We want to know who she is. On the whole, I think, I'll go to Canton with you—with your permission, of course."

"That's kind of you," Ned replied, pleased at the offer. "I can leave three of the boys on the Sea Lion and take one with me. I should be lost without that little rascal from the Bowery."

"And I'll send a file of marines on board the Sea Lion," the captain continued. "That will make all safe there. Now, about the papers. You have the packet?"

"Yes, of course."

"What does it contain?"

G. Harvey Ralphson

"Instructions which show the hand of private parties only. They completely exonerate our Government."

"And the other parties?"

"I regret that I must not mention names, sir."

"Very well," laughed the Captain. "You have performed your mission well. The slanders must now cease. But one thing more remains to be done—the meddling nation must be identified, as I have already said. We must go to Canton."

And so, leaving the Moores and Babcock safely locked in the den on board the Union and the important papers secure in the Captain's safe, Ned, accompanied by the Captain and Jimmie, set out for Canton by boat. The way was not long, and they arrived at noon, an early start having been secured.

Ned was entirely at sea in the city, but Captain Harmon had been there a number of times, and the English chop house was soon found. Next door to it was the curio shop mentioned to Ned.

The three lounged about the chop house nearly all the afternoon. The Captain was in plain clothes, and the trio seemed to be foreigners waiting for friends to come. After a long time Ned saw a man pass the chop house and turn into the curio shop who did not seem to be a Chinaman.

"Jimmie," he said to the little fellow, "suppose you go in there and buy a dragon, or a silk coat, or a tin elephant. Anything to give you a notion as to what is going on in the shop." The lad was off in a moment, and then the Captain turned to Ned.

"Why did you send the boy?" he asked.

"Because we may both be wanted outside," was the reply.

"You mean that others may come—others who should be followed and observed?"

"That's the idea," Ned replied.

Directly two more men, evidently not Chinamen, passed into the shop, then Jimmie came running out.

"They're going into a back room," he said.

Ned strolled into the shop, and in a moment the Captain followed. Jimmie remained at the door.

The two worked gradually back to the door of the rear room, and Ned "accidentally" leaned against it. It was locked. With the impact of the boy's shoulder against the panels came a scraping of chairs on the floor of the room beyond.

"You've stirred them up," whispered the Captain.

Then some one called from the inside.

"What do you want?"

"A word with you," Ned replied.

The shopkeeper now drew near and motioned the two away. When they did not obey he motioned toward the street, as if threatening to call assistance.

"Who is it?" was now asked.

"A messenger from Captain Henry Moore and his son," Ned answered, with a smile at the Captain.

There was a long pause inside.

"Where is he?" was asked.

"A prisoner. He wished me to come here."

Then the door was opened a trifle and the two saw inside. The shopkeeper, thinking that all was well, went back to the front of the shop.

When the door swung open both Ned and the Captain threw themselves against it. It went back against the wall with a bang, and the two nearly fell to the floor.

When they straightened up again they saw a servant standing between them and the still open doorway. At a round table in the back end of the apartment were three men—all Europeans.

Ned stepped forward to address them, but Captain Harmon drew him back and motioned toward the door.

"What do you want?" one of the three asked, in English. "Why this intrusion?"

Then Ned observed the face of the speaker, for the light was strong upon it. It was a face he had often seen pictured in reports of diplomatic cases. It was the face of one of the keenest diplomats in the world.

"I come from Captain Moore," Ned said, almost trembling at the thought of standing in the presence of the powerful man who had spoken.

"Can you send him here?" was asked.

"I'll try," was the reply.

"Who is your friend?" asked the other, pointing to Captain Harmon.

Ned turned toward the Captain and was amazed at the change which had taken place in his friend's appearance. The erect naval officer was no longer at his side. Instead, a shambling, bent figure stood there, with face bent to the floor.

"A seaman who is on sick leave," Ned replied.

"Well, step outside while we consider what to do in the matter," said the diplomat. "Chang!" he called.

The shopkeeper appeared at the door.

"Watch these fellows," came the orders. "Watch them, understand!"

The words were spoken in French, a language which Ned understood something of. The boy glanced keenly toward the man who had answered to the name of Chang. He decided that he was not a Chinaman.

The three stepped out into the shop together, Ned watching the seeming Chinaman closely. It was his idea that the fellow would give a signal which would call a score or more of mercenaries to his assistance. He believed that it was not the intention of the men in the rear room to let them leave the place.

When the three neared the center of the shop the alleged Chinaman lifted a whistle to his lips, as if about to signal. Ned snatched the whistle away and seized the fellow by the throat.

"Now, Captain," he whispered.

The Captain, now his old self, sprang forward and the shop-keeper was soon tied fast, gagged, and laid behind one of the counters. Then the two walked calmly out of the place.

Jimmie paused long enough to lean over the counter and make a face at the prisoner, then followed on.

"You know the truth now?" asked Ned, as the two stopped on a street corner not far away.

"Yes."

"The name of the meddlesome power is no longer a mystery?"

"Yes, I understand that, but what are we to do?"

"Make our report."

"Then you think the case is closed?" asked the Captain.

"Well," replied Ned, "we have all the documents, and we have the name of the diplomat who was waiting for Moore. What more do you want?"

"Rather a clean job of it," mused the Captain. "I wonder what the Washington people will say when the papers are laid before them; with the name of the man Moore was doing business with?"

"What will be done about it?"

"Nothing. All Uncle Sam can do is to block such games."

"And the Moores and Babcock?"

"They may be punished for attempting to wreck the Sea Lion."

"I don't like diplomatic cases," Ned said. "The rascals usually get free of punishment."

"Well," Captain Moore said, "suppose we go on board the Union while we can. As soon as the alleged shopkeeper is found behind the counter, there will be the dickens to pay. They will know that the identity of the big gun has been established, and every attempt to murder us will be made."

"You think the man knew you?" asked Ned.

"I don't know. You noticed how I changed my attitude all I could when he looked at me. I rather fancied he saw something military about me before that."

"Then we may as well go aboard," Ned said.

"You have made a wonderful success of the mission," the Captain said, that night. "You have done everything expected of you and more. Has it been easy?"

"Well," was the reply, "we have been kept busy!"

The Captain laughed and pointed to the shore of the inlet in which the Union lay.

"There are people who want to come aboard!" he said. "See the commotion on shore?"

G. Harvey Ralphson

"Shall you permit them to board?"

"Decidedly not. I have cabled to Washington for instructions. Until they arrive I shall keep everybody off the boat."

"That listens good to me," Ned said.

Boats which seemed to have no business there prowled around the warship all night, and once a sneak was caught hanging to the forward chains. However, no one succeeded in getting aboard.

In the morning the Captain came to Ned's cabin with a number of cablegrams, all from Washington.

"I have orders for you," he said.

Ned yawned and shook his head.

"Not for a submarine trip," he said.

"I am going north," the Captain said, "north through the China Sea, into the Yellow Sea, and so on to the Gulf of Pechili. Do you know where that is?"

"It is the highway to Peking," laughed Ned. "I hope you are not going there."

"Sure, and you are going with me."

"What for?" asked the boy.

"To find the two men who sat at the table with the diplomat at Canton," was the reply. "The Government wants them."

"We might have taken them, a few hours ago," mused Ned.

"Doubtful," said the Captain. "Besides, there is other work for you in the Imperial City. Your friends are going with us, and the Sea Lion is to be left here."

"And the prisoners?"

"They remain on board. In fact, the Government has a surprise for the conspirators. We may want Babcock and the Moores at Peking."

"And you'll send the papers to Washington?"

"Yes. Write your report, briefly, for they now know a lot about the wonderful success you have had."

"But how are we to get from the coast to Peking?" asked Ned. "It is quite a trip, and the diplomats will be after us."

"Motorcycles have been provided," was the reply, "and a flying squadron of my boys will go with you."

"Whoopee!" yelled Jimmie, who entered the cabin just in time to hear the latter part of the talk. "Me for the Chink land! I'll go and tell Frank and Jack."

The boy dashed off, and all preparations for the trip were made.

That night the Union sailed out of the China Sea. The case of the missing papers was closed. The gold was still at the bottom of the sea, but that was not Ned's fault. He had followed orders. However, the gold could be taken out at any time. The discovery of the men who had conspired with the famous diplomat could not wait.

What the boys did, the luck they had, and the adventures

they met with, on the way from the coast to the Imperial City, will be told in the next volume of this series, "Boy Scouts on Motorcycles; or, With the Flying Squadron."

THE END

Choose from Thousands of 1stWorldLibrary Classics By

A. M. Barnard
Ada Leverson
Adolphus William Ward
Aesop
Agatha Christie
Alexander Aaronsohn
Alexander Kielland
Alexandre Dumas
Alfred Gatty
Alfred Ollivant
Alice Duer Miller
Alice Turner Curtis
Alice Dunbar
Allen Chapman
Alleyne Ireland
Ambrose Bierce
Amelia E. Barr
Amory H. Bradford
Andrew Lang
Andrew McFarland Davis
Andy Adams
Angela Brazil
Anna Alice Chapin
Anna Sewell
Annie Besant
Annie Hamilton Donnell
Annie Payson Call
Annie Roe Carr
Annonaymous
Anton Chekhov
Archibald Lee Fletcher
Arnold Bennett
Arthur C. Benson
Arthur Conan Doyle
Arthur M. Winfield
Arthur Ransome
Arthur Schnitzler
Arthur Train
Atticus
B.H. Baden-Powell
B. M. Bower
B. C. Chatterjee
Baroness Emmuska Orczy
Baroness Orczy
Basil King
Bayard Taylor
Ben Macomber
Bertha Muzzy Bower
Bjornstjerne Bjornson

Booth Tarkington
Boyd Cable
Bram Stoker
C. Collodi
C. E. Orr
C. M. Ingleby
Carolyn Wells
Catherine Parr Traill
Charles A. Eastman
Charles Amory Beach
Charles Dickens
Charles Dudley Warner
Charles Farrar Browne
Charles Ives
Charles Kingsley
Charles Klein
Charles Hanson Towne
Charles Lathrop Pack
Charles Romyn Dake
Charles Whibley
Charles Willing Beale
Charlotte M. Braeme
Charlotte M. Yonge
Charlotte Perkins Stetson
Clair W. Hayes
Clarence Day Jr.
Clarence E. Mulford
Clemence Housman
Confucius
Coningsby Dawson
Cornelis DeWitt Wilcox
Cyril Burleigh
D. H. Lawrence
Daniel Defoe
David Garnett
Dinah Craik
Don Carlos Janes
Donald Keyhoe
Dorothy Kilner
Dougan Clark
Douglas Fairbanks
E. Nesbit
E. P. Roe
E. Phillips Oppenheim
E. S. Brooks
Earl Barnes
Edgar Rice Burroughs
Edith Van Dyne
Edith Wharton

Edward Everett Hale
Edward J. O'Biren
Edward S. Ellis
Edwin L. Arnold
Eleanor Atkins
Eleanor Hallowell Abbott
Eliot Gregory
Elizabeth Gaskell
Elizabeth McCracken
Elizabeth Von Arnim
Ellem Key
Emerson Hough
Emilie F. Carlen
Emily Bronte
Emily Dickinson
Enid Bagnold
Enilor Macartney Lane
Erasmus W. Jones
Ernie Howard Pie
Ethel May Dell
Ethel Turner
Ethel Watts Mumford
Eugene Sue
Eugenie Foa
Eugene Wood
Eustace Hale Ball
Evelyn Everett-green
Everard Cotes
F. H. Cheley
F. J. Cross
F. Marion Crawford
Fannie E. Newberry
Federick Austin Ogg
Ferdinand Ossendowski
Fergus Hume
Florence A. Kilpatrick
Fremont B. Deering
Francis Bacon
Francis Darwin
Frances Hodgson Burnett
Frances Parkinson Keyes
Frank Gee Patchin
Frank Harris
Frank Jewett Mather
Frank L. Packard
Frank V. Webster
Frederic Stewart Isham
Frederick Trevor Hill
Frederick Winslow Taylor

Friedrich Kerst	Hayden Carruth	James Branch Cabell
Friedrich Nietzsche	Helent Hunt Jackson	James DeMille
Fyodor Dostoyevsky	Helen Nicolay	James Joyce
G.A. Henty	Hendrik Conscience	James Lane Allen
G.K. Chesterton	Hendy David Thoreau	James Lane Allen
Gabrielle E. Jackson	Henri Barbusse	James Oliver Curwood
Garrett P. Serviss	Henrik Ibsen	James Oppenheim
Gaston Leroux	Henry Adams	James Otis
George A. Warren	Henry Ford	James R. Driscoll
George Ade	Henry Frost	Jane Abbott
Geroge Bernard Shaw	Henry James	Jane Austen
George Cary Eggleston	Henry Jones Ford	Jane L. Stewart
George Durston	Henry Seton Merriman	Janet Aldridge
George Ebers	Henry W Longfellow	Jens Peter Jacobsen
George Eliot	Herbert A. Giles	Jerome K. Jerome
George Gissing	Herbert Carter	Jessie Graham Flower
George MacDonald	Herbert N. Casson	John Buchan
George Meredith	Herman Hesse	John Burroughs
George Orwell	Hildegard G. Frey	John Cournos
George Sylvester Viereck	Homer	John F. Kennedy
George Tucker	Honore De Balzac	John Gay
George W. Cable	Horace B. Day	John Glasworthy
George Wharton James	Horace Walpole	John Habberton
Gertrude Atherton	Horatio Alger Jr.	John Joy Bell
Gordon Casserly	Howard Pyle	John Kendrick Bangs
Grace E. King	Howard R. Garis	John Milton
Grace Gallatin	Hugh Lofting	John Philip Sousa
Grace Greenwood	Hugh Walpole	John Taintor Foote
Grant Allen	Humphry Ward	Jonas Lauritz Idemil Lie
Guillermo A. Sherwell	Ian Maclaren	Jonathan Swift
Gulielma Zollinger	Inez Haynes Gillmore	Joseph A. Altsheler
Gustav Flaubert	Irving Bacheller	Joseph Carey
H. A. Cody	Isabel Cecilia Williams	Joseph Conrad
H. B. Irving	Isabel Hornibrook	Joseph E. Badger Jr
H. C. Bailey	Israel Abrahams	Joseph Hergesheimer
H. G. Wells	Ivan Turgenev	Joseph Jacobs
H. H. Munro	J. G.Austin	Jules Vernes
H. Irving Hancock	J. Henri Fabre	Julian Hawthrone
H. R. Naylor	J. M. Barrie	Julie A Lippmann
H. Rider Haggard	J. M. Walsh	Justin Huntly McCarthy
H. W. C. Davis	J. Macdonald Oxley	Kakuzo Okakura
Haldeman Julius	J. R. Miller	Karle Wilson Baker
Hall Caine	J. S. Fletcher	Kate Chopin
Hamilton Wright Mabie	J. S. Knowles	Kenneth Grahame
Hans Christian Andersen	J. Storer Clouston	Kenneth McGaffey
Harold Avery	J. W. Duffield	Kate Langley Bosher
Harold McGrath	Jack London	Kate Langley Bosher
Harriet Beecher Stowe	Jacob Abbott	Katherine Cecil Thurston
Harry Castlemon	James Allen	Katherine Stokes
Harry Coghill	James Andrews	L. A. Abbot
Harry Houidini	James Baldwin	L. T. Meade

L. Frank Baum
Latta Griswold
Laura Dent Crane
Laura Lee Hope
Laurence Housman
Lawrence Beasley
Leo Tolstoy
Leonid Andreyev
Lewis Carroll
Lewis Sperry Chafer
Lilian Bell
Lloyd Osbourne
Louis Hughes
Louis Joseph Vance
Louis Tracy
Louisa May Alcott
Lucy Fitch Perkins
Lucy Maud Montgomery
Luther Benson
Lydia Miller Middleton
Lyndon Orr
M. Corvus
M. H. Adams
Margaret E. Sangster
Margret Howth
Margaret Vandercook
Margaret W. Hungerford
Margret Penrose
Maria Edgeworth
Maria Thompson Daviess
Mariano Azuela
Marion Polk Angellotti
Mark Overton
Mark Twain
Mary Austin
Mary Catherine Crowley
Mary Cole
Mary Hastings Bradley
Mary Roberts Rinehart
Mary Rowlandson
M. Wollstonecraft Shelley
Maud Lindsay
Max Beerbohm
Myra Kelly
Nathaniel Hawthrone
Nicolo Machiavelli
O. F. Walton
Oscar Wilde
Owen Johnson
P.G. Wodehouse
Paul and Mabel Thorne

Paul G. Tomlinson
Paul Severing
Percy Brebner
Percy Keese Fitzhugh
Peter B. Kyne
Plato
Quincy Allen
R. Derby Holmes
R. L. Stevenson
R. S. Ball
Rabindranath Tagore
Rahul Alvares
Ralph Bonehill
Ralph Henry Barbour
Ralph Victor
Ralph Waldo Emmerson
Rene Descartes
Ray Cummings
Rex Beach
Rex E. Beach
Richard Harding Davis
Richard Jefferies
Richard Le Gallienne
Robert Barr
Robert Frost
Robert Gordon Anderson
Robert L. Drake
Robert Lansing
Robert Lynd
Robert Michael Ballantyne
Robert W. Chambers
Rosa Nouchette Carey
Rudyard Kipling
Saint Augustine
Samuel B. Allison
Samuel Hopkins Adams
Sarah Bernhardt
Sarah C. Hallowell
Selma Lagerlof
Sherwood Anderson
Sigmund Freud
Standish O'Grady
Stanley Weyman
Stella Benson
Stella M. Francis
Stephen Crane
Stewart Edward White
Stijn Streuvels
Swami Abhedananda
Swami Parmananda
T. S. Ackland

T. S. Arthur
The Princess Der Ling
Thomas A. Janvier
Thomas A Kempis
Thomas Anderton
Thomas Bailey Aldrich
Thomas Bulfinch
Thomas De Quincey
Thomas Dixon
Thomas H. Huxley
Thomas Hardy
Thomas More
Thornton W. Burgess
U. S. Grant
Upton Sinclair
Valentine Williams
Various Authors
Vaughan Kester
Victor Appleton
Victor G. Durham
Victoria Cross
Virginia Woolf
Wadsworth Camp
Walter Camp
Walter Scott
Washington Irving
Wilbur Lawton
Wilkie Collins
Willa Cather
Willard F. Baker
William Dean Howells
William le Queux
W. Makepeace Thackeray
William W. Walter
William Shakespeare
Winston Churchill
Yei Theodora Ozaki
Yogi Ramacharaka
Young E. Allison
Zane Grey